ROMEO & HER SISTER

by Jillian Blevins

GHOST LIGHT PUBLICATIONS

ROMEO AND HER SISTER

SPECIAL NOTE

Anyone receiving permission to produce ROMEO & HER SISTER is required to give credit to the Author as sole and exclusive Author of the Play on the title page of all programs distributed in connection with performances of the Play and in all instances in which the title of the Play appears for purposes of advertising, publicizing or otherwise exploiting the Play and/or a production thereof. The name of the Author must appear on a separate line, in which no other name appears, immediately beneath the title and in size of type equal to 50% of the size of the largest, most prominent letter used for the title of the Play. No person, firm, or entity may receive credit larger or more prominent than that accorded the Author.

SPECIAL NOTE ON SONGS AND RECORDINGS

For performances of copyrighted songs, arrangements or recordings mentioned in these Plays, the permission of the copyright owner(s) must be obtained. Other songs, arrangements or recordings may be substituted provided permission from the copyright owner(s) of such songs, arrangements or recordings is obtained; or songs, arrangements or recordings in the public domain may be substituted.

Cover Art and Book Design: A.C. Daniel & Jonathan Cook
(art based on Times article)
First Edition: March 2026
ISBN 978-1-964045-14-6

ROMEO & HER SISTER received its World premiere at New Hampshire Theatre Project in Portsmouth, New Hampshire in June 2024.

The cast was as follows:

CHARLOTTE CUSHMAN .... Amy Desrosiers

SUSAN CUSHMAN .... Greta Swartz

SALLIE MERCER .... Seda Tuncok

MATILDA HAYS .... Annie Stone

EDWIN FORREST .... Michael Towle

BENJAMIN WEBSTER .... Tim Young

ELEANORA .... Corrie Owens-Beauchesne

The crew was as follows:

DIRECTOR .... Courtney St. Gelais

SET DESIGN .... Joshua Goldberg

SOUND DESIGN .... Courtney St. Gelais

LIGHTING DESIGN .... Kevin McDonough

COSTUMES .... Jen Towle

FIGHT CHOREOGRAPHY .... Jen Towle

INTIMACY COORDINATOR .... Samantha Griffin

STAGE MANAGER(S) .... Jess Gero

.... Michelle Levine

.... Jay Doane

ROMEO AND HER SISTER

CHARACTERS

CHARLOTTE CUSHMAN

she/her. Early 30's. Tall, masculine, and intense. Beautiful speaking voice, powerful presence. A star. American.*

SUSAN CUSHMAN

she/her. Early to mid 20's. Charlotte's sister, delicate and pretty. The mother of eight-year-old Ned, her scandalous marriage to a man in his 70's has been dissolved. Effervescent and charming and a little bratty. American.

SALLIE MERCER

she/her. Early to mid 20's. A free Black woman, brainy, bright and outspoken to a fault. Charlotte's assistant, dresser, and closest confidant. American.

MATILDA HAYS

she/her. Mid 20's to early 30's. Bookish and mousy. A journalist, translator of French, and a failed actress. Charlotte's lover. Sometimes called Max. English.

EDWIN FORREST

he/him. 30's or 40's. An actor. Pompous and bombastic, with a professional grudge against Charlotte. Tall, handsome, imposing, and extremely American.

BENJAMIN WEBSTER

he/him. 50+. Manager of London's Royal Haymarket Theatre. Anxious and polite. English.

ELEANORA

she/her. Late teens to early 20's. An ardent fan of Charlotte's, and an aspiring actress. Pretty and a bit dim. English.

TIME AND PLACE

December 1845. London. The stage and dressing room of the Haymarket Theatre, a grand and well-appointed Victorian playhouse, and another dressing room at the equally prestigious Princess' Theatre.

NOTES

The pace is fast, and the tone is comic (think Oscar Wilde). Anachronism is purposeful, but time and place remain squarely in 19th century London.

Words in CAPITAL letters are more infused with feeling than those in italics, which are merely emphasized.

Verse is not a "break in reality" from the rest of the play, but an opportunity for the character to confide in the audience; the world of the play remains consistent throughout.

*CHARLOTTE's pronouns are she/her–but non-binary and trans actors can and should be considered to play her, and to tell her story through the lens of their own experience.

ACT 1

PROLOGUE

SALLIE. Two sisters, unalike in every way,
    In gloomy London, where we lay our scene.
    They nurse their ancient grudge, rehearse a play,
    And keep their ru'nous scandals still unseen.
    Their rivalry for fame, for wealth, for love
    Hath poisoned both the sisters all their life;
    The elder evermore her worth must prove,
    The younger wishes most to be a wife.
    The only way this coil may–
SUSAN. Miss Mercer! Stop!
SALLIE. What?
SUSAN. The play's only just begun and you're about to give
    away the ending!
SALLIE. It's the Prologue.
SUSAN. Such a silly convention. Let's leave them in some
    suspense.
SALLIE. Forgive me, Miss Cushman, but I don't work for
    you, I work for your sister.
SUSAN. Of course. My sister. The sensational Charlotte
    Cushman. My sister, my sister, my sister–
SALLIE. She's waiting for you.
SUSAN. Please. Sallie. I need a respite from this drudgery.

I'm going mad with boredom speaking the same words day after day–

SALLIE. Rehearsing.

SUSAN. And all this rehearsal has left me with no time to meet a single suitor here in England.

SALLIE.I think we both know suitors should be the furthest thing from your mind. After the unhappy matter with Mr. Merriman–

SUSAN. Do NOT speak that vile old man's name in my presence.

SALLIE. He's your husband.

SUSAN. Not any longer. He made certain of that after he refused to die as promised, abandoning me with his son to raise and without the comforts I was due. The shame is nearly as terrible as never having married at all.

SALLIE. Suitors are what got you into this mess, and your sister is what's gotten you out of it. You might show a bit more gratitude.

SUSAN. Ah yes. Gratitude. I must always be GRATEFUL to dear Charlotte for saving our fatherless family from disaster and dragging me onstage to act in her shadow. I can never for a moment forget the debt I owe her. All that GRATITUDE is stifling.

SALLIE. She cares for you.

SUSAN. Mother and I were quite cared for by her money. She needn't have carted me off to London to spend hours a day in a dark theatre.

SALLIE. Well, you're here now, aren't you? Boston will still be there when the play has ended, and you'll be returning quite a bit richer.

SUSAN. I'd much rather marry into riches. Earning one's own is so sordid.

SALLIE. Some of us feel lucky to be able to earn money for

our work at all.

SUSAN. Oh, for heaven's sake, Sallie, you were born a free woman–

SALLIE. And so were you. And you freely married a man who gave you a child, freely accepted Miss Charlotte's offer to bring you forward in New York, freely accepted her money, and freely agreed to join her in London and to play Juliet. A role any actress would kill for. So get dressed and meet her in the theatre in five minutes.

SUSAN. Aren't you supposed to help me dress?

SALLIE. I'm Charlotte's dresser. Perhaps you'll have your own one day. Until then, you'll have to manage.

(Without waiting for a response, Sallie exits.)

SUSAN. I never!

(blowing a raspberry)

TTTTHHHHHBBBBBPPPPPTTTT!

(Changing into her rehearsal skirts:)

Come to London, Susan. Get dressed, Susan. Play Juliet Susan. "A role any actress would kill for." Ugh.

(She takes a deep breath. Is she good enough to do this? She tries out a line, uncertainly.)

Romeo, Romeo, wherefore art thou–

(Sallie returns. Startled, Susan hides the mirror behind her back.)

SALLIE. Miss Cushman is indisposed and will have to postpone the rehearsal for a few hours.

SUSAN. You must be joking.

SALLIE. She'll send for you at the apartment when she's ready.

SUSAN. I'm not a parcel to be picked up whenever she likes!

SALLIE. No, miss, you're an actress. Perhaps you'd better

get used to it.
(Susan stalks off, incensed.)

SCENE 1

Charlotte in her dressing room. It is clearly the dressing room of a star. She's speaking to Webster, the theatre manager.

CHARLOTTE. I'm not sure I quite understand your concerns.

WEBSTER. Well, erm, you see, Miss Cushman, the play is due to open in just over a week –

CHARLOTTE. I'm aware of that.

WEBSTER. And of course we're honored to have you play Romeo here at the Haymarket, I mean, you received such reviews for the role in America, and your Fazio here in London was–well, the Herald called you "the greatest of actresses", and–

CHARLOTTE. I've read my notices, Mr. Webster. The problem?

WEBSTER. It's your sister.

CHARLOTTE. What about her?

WEBSTER. Well, I can't help but notice that, well, erm, she doesn't quite seem… she hasn't… I'm afraid she isn't…

CHARLOTTE. I hope you'll finish at least one sentence before this conversation has ended.

WEBSTER. *(in a rush)* She hasn't memorized any of her lines.

CHARLOTTE. And?

WEBSTER. And she's playing Juliet.

CHARLOTTE. I'll never get used to the English inclination to say everything but what one really means.

WEBSTER. I'm so sorry, Miss Cushman. I don't mean to be impertinent or to waste your time. It's just… I'm concerned that Miss Cushman–that is, the other Miss Cushman–that your sister may not be quite ready to perform by the time we open the play.

CHARLOTTE. And what do you suggest we do?

WEBSTER. Perhaps… perhaps another actress might… is there someone else who could…?

CHARLOTTE. What am I, Mr. Webster?

WEBSTER. What…? Erm… you're…. the most famous actress in America!

CHARLOTTE. I'm the most famous woman in the world.

WEBSTER. Yes. Yes, quite right.

CHARLOTTE. Do you know what people did the last time I went back to Boston?

WEBSTER. I–

CHARLOTTE. They threw me a parade. They pasted up bills that said "Welcome home, Charlotte". The papers called it CUSHMANIA.

WEBSTER. Miss Cushman…?

CHARLOTTE. I'm a star, Mr. Webster. And I can enact Romeo wherever I please. Shall I go home to Boston? Perhaps a revival in New York? Paris is lovely this time of year.

WEBSTER. Miss Cushman–

CHARLOTTE. I'm not sure you realize what a privilege it is to host the Cushman sisters for this engagement. "Sisters! Playing the greatest lovers of the literary canon! Women enacting passionate love as only two women can!" And the most famous woman in the world with top billing. We'll draw full houses no matter which theatre we play in. If you would prefer that we fill those houses elsewhere–

WEBSTER. No! No, you're quite right. Please forgive me.

CHARLOTTE. Susan will perform next week. I'll have no other Juliet.

WEBSTER. Of course.

CHARLOTTE. Until then, you will kindly stay out of the rehearsal hall and let us work.

WEBSTER. Yes.

(A pause.)

CHARLOTTE. Anything else?

WEBSTER. Oh! No, I… Right. Well.

(He leaves. Charlotte breathes a deep sigh of frustration –or satisfaction?–and Eleanora, an attractive young woman, pops up from beneath her chaise lounge.)

ELEANORA. I thought he'd never leave!

(She flings herself at Charlotte and they kiss passionately. She settles herself in Charlotte's lap.)

CHARLOTTE. That's enough, pet. I will eventually have to rehearse at this rehearsal. My sister's been waiting.

ELEANORA. Oh, just a little more time, please? You promised you'd give me acting lessons.

CHARLOTTE. Oh! Yes. Of course. Acting lessons. But not today. I have to focus on opening the play next week…

ELEANORA. I still can't believe I'm in CHARLOTTE CUSHMAN'S dressing room.

CHARLOTTE. Neither can I.

(They kiss some more.)

ELEANORA. Can you please do Hamlet for me just one more time?

CHARLOTTE. Oh, no, I couldn't…

ELEANORA. Oh, please!

CHARLOTTE. Eleanora–

ELEANORA. You know what it does to me to hear you speak those words!

CHARLOTTE. All right, all right, pet. But you must leave afterwards or else I'll get no work done all day, and there will be no Romeo next week. You do want to see me play Romeo, don't you?

ELEANORA. Oh, more than anything, Charlotte! But first– Hamlet. Please.

(Charlotte relents. We see something in her change. Her face radiates intensity and light. Her voice is rich and deep. She becomes Hamlet.)

CHARLOTTE. To be, or not to be- that is the question:

Whether 'tis nobler in the mind to suffer

The slings and arrows of outrageous fortune

Or to take arms against a sea of troubles,

And by opposing end them. To die- to sleep-

No more;

(Eleanora sighs adoringly, and Charlotte turns her attention fully towards her, the soliloquy transforming into a seduction.)

–and by a sleep to say we end

(placing her hand on Eleanora's bosom)

The heartache

and the thousand natural shocks

That flesh is heir to. 'Tis a consummation

Devoutly to be wish'd. To die- to sleep.

To sleep- perchance to dream: ay, there's the rub!

(She rubs Eleanora meaningfully.)

For in that sleep of death what dreams may come–

(Eleanora moans, unable to restrain herself any longer, and showers Charlotte with kisses.)

ELEANORA. OH! I can barely stand it! I still remember the first time I saw you play Hamlet, I was only fourteen–

CHARLOTTE. Oh, please don't say that. It makes me feel grotesquely old.

ELEANORA. And I thought 'she is a finer man than any real man I've ever met.'

CHARLOTTE. Good thing. I've always been only a passable woman.

ELEANORA. Oh, stop! You're… beautiful.

CHARLOTTE. I am very many things, Eleanora dear, but beautiful is not one of them. Now hurry along. You promised you wouldn't distract me any longer.

ELEANORA. Handsome then. All right, I'll go.

CHARLOTTE. Don't forget to leave through the back door.

ELEANORA. Charlotte?

CHARLOTTE. Yes, pet?

ELEANORA. You didn't mean that thing you said to Mr. Webster, did you?

CHARLOTTE. What thing was that?

ELEANORA. The thing about Susan being the only Juliet you'd play with?

(A pause)

Because you told me–you promised–that when you left London to tour the provinces that I would be your Juliet.

(A pause.)

You do remember?

CHARLOTTE. Yes. Yes! Of course I do. That was just a little bluster to get the old fool to stay out of my way. You have so much to learn about the theatre business, pet.

ELEANORA. How fortunate I am to have such a formidable teacher.

(They kiss.)

CHARLOTTE. *(swatting Eleanora on the behind)* Out the back.

(Eleanora squeals in surprise and leaves out a back door as Sallie comes in through the front.)

CHARLOTTE. Send for my sister now, Sallie.

SALLIE. Miss Hays is here.

CHARLOTTE. Here! But she was to be in Paris through the end of the month!

SALLIE. I take it you're seeing visitors while she's gone? Where is she? Is she dressed at least?

CHARLOTTE. Not helpful.

SALLIE. It wasn't meant to be. Shall I send her in?

CHARLOTTE. *(glancing towards the back door)* Of course. Tell her I'm ecstatic to see her.

(Sallie leaves.)

CHARLOTTE. "He that hath the steerage of my course, direct my sail." Shit.

(In walks Matilda Hayes, dressed nearly identically to Charlotte with a handsome waistcoat and elegant bow tie over her skirts, but somehow the effect isn't the same. She throws herself at Charlotte.)

MATILDA. My darling! I've missed you so terribly!

CHARLOTTE. Matilda! My love, what brings you back to London? And so soon?

MATILDA. Oh, I was sitting there in that little flat poring over those George Sand texts, and I should have been thrilled–it was Paris, and the English Ladies' Journal was paying for everything, and I was working on translating these fantastic writings–but I was just miserable because I wasn't with you! And I thought, how can I possibly miss Charlotte playing Romeo in London? I can't! And so here I am.

CHARLOTTE. But… your work on the Sand manuscripts?

MATILDA. I can translate right here! The estate let me travel with the texts. Isn't that wonderful? Now I can be right beside you all the time!

(They embrace. We see Charlotte's grimace over Matilda's shoulder.)

CHARLOTTE. Oh, Max! How wonderful.

MATILDA. I got your letters. Charlotte, they were so beautiful. "My dearest friend, I long for you every moment since we've been parted; I see your face floating before me as I fall asleep."

CHARLOTTE. You memorized them?

MATILDA. I keep them with me always! They're part of the reason I had to return! Some of them were… quite descriptive.

CHARLOTTE. Oh?

MATILDA. I'm not the only one who has a way with words.

(They kiss passionately.)

CHARLOTTE. Oh, I have missed you, Max. Truly.

MATILDA. Now, I must take you to lunch at once.

CHARLOTTE. Darling, I can't.

MATILDA. But surely you must be due for a break by now.

CHARLOTTE. We haven't started yet.

MATILDA. You haven't? But what have you been doing all day?

CHARLOTTE. There have been some… struggles with Susan.

MATILDA. For goodness sake. Why don't you send your spoiled sister home to mummy and hire a real actress?

CHARLOTTE. Like you?

MATILDA. *(flushing)* That's not what I meant. You know I don't do that anymore. I'm much too quiet, and too plain, and…

CHARLOTTE. And you've already met me.

MATILDA. Exactly. It was our destiny to meet, and because of my horrible, ill-fated foray onto the stage, we have. And now I can spend my time supporting your genius.

CHARLOTTE. Susan will be fine. It's important that she be my Juliet. Sisterly love is pure. It will stop any… talk.

MATILDA. There's been talk?

CHARLOTTE. Just the usual rumblings. That I'm somehow too real of a man, my stage love for women too convincing.

MATILDA. How foolish. Would these gossips prefer a bad actress?

CHARLOTTE. It's Forrest, I'm certain of it. He arrived in town from New Orleans, and then the whispers began.

MATILDA. I despise that pompous, loathsome man.

CHARLOTTE. And he despises me. Ever since we played together in New York and I received glowing notices and he was savaged in the press.

MATILDA. "Milquetoast", they called him, wasn't it?

CHARLOTTE. But it was no fault of mine!

MATILDA. Well.

CHARLOTTE. Well, what?

MATILDA. You did decide to play Hamlet just after his opened.

CHARLOTTE. Every great tragedian must try their hand at Hamlet. Booth played him at the same time as both of us!

MATILDA. And your last Romeo played at the same time as his as well.

CHARLOTTE. I had no idea!

MATILDA. And last time you were both in London he switched from Brutus to Antony and you did too?

(A pause.)

CHARLOTTE. And I outshone and outsold him every time!

(They laugh.)

All right. So he has good reason to hate me. But I won't let him destroy my reputation here in London with petty rumors. That's why I need Susan. To remind my audience that I'm a paragon of virtue.

MATILDA. And so you are.

CHARLOTTE. Chaste and pure as the driven snow. No one will ever see me with any man, they'll continue to assume my incorruptible maidenhood–

MATILDA. And so our friendship is beyond reproach.

CHARLOTTE. So it is.

(They kiss.)

Now my darling, you must be off. If I'm to get any work at all done today I can't have you here distracting me.

MATILDA. Of course. I'll see you tonight. I'm so excited to be here with you again and to see your Romeo at last! I'm even excited to meet your coddled little sister.

CHARLOTTE. Matilda.

MATILDA. Charlotte.

CHARLOTTE. *(gently)* We've discussed this. It wouldn't be wise for you two to meet.

MATILDA. You're ashamed of me.

CHARLOTTE. No. I'm not. Max. Believe me, it's only out of love for you that I want to keep you apart.

MATILDA. I can be discreet.

CHARLOTTE. It's not a question of your discretion–

MATILDA. No, it's a question of your pride–

CHARLOTTE. Here we go–

MATILDA. You're a tyrant! You control your mother and your sister with your money, managers and financiers with your fame, and everyone else with your sheer… Charlotte-ness. And I'm a fool to imagine that I might be any different.

CHARLOTTE. Please, I told you I need to work. Let's not fight.

MATILDA. You're right. And do you know? I have to work too. I'm terribly behind on my writing for the Journal, and I only have so much time before I have to return all the Sand manuscripts to the estate, so perhaps it would be best if I stayed at my own flat this week after all.

CHARLOTTE. Dearest–

MATILDA. Good luck with your rehearsals. And with Susan.

CHARLOTTE. Max!

MATILDA. I'll stay out of your way. Sorry to have bothered you.

CHARLOTTE. Please, don't leave this way.

MATILDA. What you mean is, please leave, but don't make a fuss. All right. I'll leave quietly. Just pretend I was never here. Just… pretend I'm still in Paris.
(She leaves.)

CHARLOTTE. Is love a tender thing? It is too rough,

Too rude, too boisterous. It pricks like a thorn.

Ain't it the truth.

SALLIE. *(entering)* Your sister is ready to rehearse, Miss Cushman.

CHARLOTTE. Is she really?

SALLIE. Well, she's here.

CHARLOTTE. That sounds more like it.

SALLIE. Let's get you changed.

CHARLOTTE. "Once more, into the breech…es."
(*Sallie begins dressing Charlotte in her rehearsal clothes.*)

SALLIE. Arms up. Do you want my opinion?

CHARLOTTE. Would it stop you if I said no?

SALLIE. Turn. Mr. Webster wasn't wrong about Susan. Aside from the lines, she seems to loathe every moment of the play. Last night she tried to hurl herself from the balcony.

CHARLOTTE. Thank goodness for the Nurse's quick reflexes.

SALLIE. Left foot. Now, right.

CHARLOTTE. *(stepping into her trousers)* There I am.

SALLIE. Every inch a Romeo. Susan, on the other hand… Surely she can be replaced, even at this late hour?

CHARLOTTE. I pay you a good salary, don't I Sallie?

SALLIE. Better than anyone else in my position. Not nearly what I deserve.

CHARLOTTE. And what do you do with that salary? Besides buy books.

SALLIE. I send it back home to my mother and my brothers in Philadelphia.

CHARLOTTE. And so have I, for my mother and sister. For nearly half my life, I've sent them money, every month, kept them out of the poorhouse. I've been the man of my mother's house since I was sixteen. And I've never gotten a word of thanks from either of them. Nor a word of congratulations for my success. They don't see what the world sees, only a strange and unlovely person with an open checkbook.

SALLIE. So why bring her here?

CHARLOTTE. I need to unyoke myself from the both of them. I'll endure my sister for the run of Romeo, so that

I'll never have to again.

SALLIE. I don't follow.

CHARLOTTE. Once I've made her a star, she can go her own way. Let her pay the bills for a while.

SALLIE. And you think Juliet will make her a star.

CHARLOTTE. If she finally relents and allows us to take her in hand in the next seven days? I do.

SALLIE. Well then. We'd better get to work.

SCENE 2

Charlotte and Susan are rehearsing. Sallie stands in the wings with a prompt book.

CHARLOTTE. If I profane with my unworthiest hand
    This holy shrine, the gentle sin is this:
    My lips, two blushing pilgrims, ready stand
    To smooth that rough touch with a tender kiss.
SUSAN. Good pilgrim, you do… wrong?
    You do wrong your hand too much,
    Which…
    (She glances towards the wings.)
SALLIE. "Mannerly devotion."
SUSAN. …which mannerly devotion shows in this; for…
CHARLOTTE. *(quickly finishing her line, impatient)* "For
    saints have hands that pilgrims' hands do touch, and
    palm to palm is holy palmers' kiss."
    (Back to Romeo.)
    Have not saints lips, and holy palmers too?
SUSAN. Um… Yes?
CHARLOTTE. O, then, dear saint, let lips do what hands do;
    They pray, grant thou, lest faith turn to despair.
SUSAN. I forget.
CHARLOTTE. Then ask Sallie for a line.
SUSAN. No, I forget all of it. Not only the words. Where

I'm supposed to stand, the dancing, how I'm supposed to hold my arms…

CHARLOTTE. Susan. You can do this. You haven't forgotten.

SUSAN. I think I need a break.

CHARLOTTE. We've only been rehearsing for a quarter of an hour!

SUSAN. Well that's certainly not my fault. I've been waiting all day–

SALLIE. Then why weren't you practicing your lines?

SUSAN. Because I'm BORED, Sallie!

CHARLOTTE. Bored. You're rehearsing for one of the greatest plays in the English language, in one of the greatest cities in the world, opposite the biggest star in the world–

SUSAN. Ha!

CHARLOTTE. –whatever you think of me, opposite a very good actress. The situation you are in is–the opposite of boring!

SUSAN. I haven't been to a single party, or even a proper dinner with anyone interesting since we arrived here. It's only been you, Ned, and this damned play.

CHARLOTTE. I've invited you to dine with my friends.

SUSAN. Eating soup with old spinsters and no men is not my idea of a party! You've never had the taste for good society. Or the looks.

CHARLOTTE. My friends are some of the greatest writers and artists in Europe!

SUSAN. "The jolly bachelors"? Pretentious, homely ladies with no husbands or children or place in good society!

CHARLOTTE. I'm sorry that you're too frivolous and empty-headed to appreciate great minds and would rather surround yourself with preening dandies–

SUSAN. *(whining)* I just want to go home! I can't stand it here. I can't stand the damp and the fog, I can't stand this dusty old theatre, I can't stand this interminable play, and I can't stand you!

SALLIE. Let's take five.

CHARLOTTE. Susan. What's happened? You haven't always hated the stage this much. I thought you'd love playing Juliet.

SUSAN. Yes, with a real Romeo, I would.

CHARLOTTE. A "real Romeo"?

SUSAN. Yes.

CHARLOTTE. *(very slowly, as if to a child)* Susie. You do understand that… acting is… pretending, don't you?

SUSAN. I mean a real MAN.

CHARLOTTE. Ah yes, it's always about that for you, isn't it?

SUSAN. Someone handsome, someone I could feel something for–

CHARLOTTE. You mean someone you could flirt with?

SUSAN. Just because you're hopelessly frigid, it doesn't mean I have to be.

SALLIE. Should I get some coffee?

CHARLOTTE. *(together)* No!

SUSAN. *(together)* Yes!

If I'm to pretend to fall in love, I want it to be with a man.

CHARLOTTE. Like that insufferable Edwin Forrest, you mean?

SUSAN. Well, yes, maybe!

CHARLOTTE. A blowhard who's more interested in his own reflection in the mirror–

SUSAN. When little girls dream of being Juliet, they don't

dream of their sister standing under the balcony.

CHARLOTTE. If I were a "real" man, we wouldn't have booked this engagement at all. If I were a "real" man, propriety would demand that we barely even touch onstage, just gesture in each other's general direction. If I were a "real" man, this would be like every other dull, insipid, sexless Romeo and Juliet anyone has ever seen.

(A pause, as Susan considers this.)

Susan, don't you see? This will be more like your fantasies than it ever could with a man playing Romeo. That's why people are clamoring to see you. Because they know that, as sisters, you will be allowed to get closer to the truth of love than any other Romeo and Juliet they've ever seen. You need to trust me. You can be great. I know you can be great. Let me make you great.

SUSAN. Why?

CHARLOTTE. What?

SUSAN. Why do you care? Why do you want me to "be great"?

CHARLOTTE. Because you're my sister.

SUSAN. Yes, your motivations are always so pure. Like the time you brought me to the opening of that opera, I was only eleven, and you still had your singing voice–

CHARLOTTE. Figaro? This again?

SUSAN. I was so excited. I had a new dress, and I was going to meet all the important people you'd been spending time with. I was ready.

CHARLOTTE. I wasn't even seventeen years old, you can't possibly blame me for–

SUSAN. And you dragged me around the party telling the same sad story over and over. How father had lost all our money, and came home with nothing but stale bread for us to chew on, and then stopped coming home altogether. How we'd moved six times, each place more squalid than the last. How mother had opened that pathetic boarding house and I was spending my days washing filthy linens and cleaning toilets–

CHARLOTTE. It was all true!

SUSAN. You humiliated me! I wasn't a guest, I was a prop. Charlotte's pitiable little sister, there to illustrate your maudlin tale of woe. And there you were, starring in an opera out of the goodness of your heart. Not because you wanted applause, or to be looked at. No, being in the spotlight was a sacrifice you were making for the silly little girl in the stupid, fancy dress.

CHARLOTTE. I bought you that dress.

SUSAN. You're not as good an actress as you think, Charlotte. You may have everyone else fooled, but every time you do something "generous" for someone else, it's always really for you. I'd respect you much more if you'd admit it.

CHARLOTTE. For Ned then.

SUSAN. Fine, be that way. Keep up the good sister charade. I'll do your show.

SALLIE. Fantastic. Let's get back to it, then.

SUSAN. I may even be great. But when this is over, so are we, Charlotte.

CHARLOTTE. Another grand proclamation? I've heard this one before–

SALLIE. We're wasting valuable time–

SUSAN. I mean it–

CHARLOTTE. –but you always come crawling back for another handout.

SUSAN. And you LOVE it!

SALLIE. Enough! You're no better than squabbling school

girls!

CHARLOTTE. I'll tell you what, Susie. I would love nothing more than to be "done". I have a good life here in Europe. I have friends. People are more interesting and open-minded and all the Puritans left three hundred years ago. The only thing bringing me back to Boston is my obligation to the three of you, which I'm frankly just as exhausted by as you are. Just say the word and you'll never see me again. But I swear to God, if you don't start actually trying to play Juliet – show up to rehearsal on time, pretend you like me, and memorize your GODDAMNED LINES – I will make sure you are never rid of me, and that your social life consists of me, Sallie, your eight year old, and a dozen more dusty old theaters. You want me out of your life? Do. Your. Job.

(A pause.)

SUSAN. Sallie. Where were we?

SALLIE. "Saints do not move…"

SUSAN. *(with more commitment than we've seen so far)* Saints do not move, though grant for prayers' sake.

CHARLOTTE. Then move not, while my prayer's effect I take.

(Charlotte moves to kiss Susan, who deflects. Over the following, Susan earnestly tries to act while also avoiding Charlotte's increasingly insistent touch.)

You're to let me kiss you here!

SUSAN. No thanks.

(A physical struggle as Charlotte attempts to kiss Susan, who resists.)

CHARLOTTE. Thus from my lips, by yours, my sin is purged.

SUSAN. Then have my lips the sin that they have took. Stop it!

CHARLOTTE. Sin from thy lips? O trespass sweetly urged! Give me–my sin–again.

(Charlotte tries again; Susan punches her, with surprising force.)

SUSAN. *(savagely)* You kiss by the book. *(looking right at a dazed Charlotte)* Sallie, tell Miss Cushman that I'm going back home to see Ned, and to memorize my goddamned lines.

(Susan exists. Sallie and Charlotte look after her, then to each other.)

SALLIE. *(meaning it)* She's good.

SCENE 3

Sallie and Susan on the stage. Susan stands center, while Sallie is off to the side holding a book.

SALLIE. Fear.

(Susan turns her face to the side, covering her mouth with one hand.)

Silent sorrow.

(Susan folds her arms and raises them to her forehead.)

Hopelessness.

(Susan tilts her head to the left and drapes her left arm across it, fingers limply hanging to the right of her face.)

Oops, almost. Switch sides.

SUSAN. Oh, pooh!

(She tilts her head to the right and drapes her right arm across it.)

SALLIE. Grief.

(Susan hangs her head and covers her face.)

SALLIE. Good, but-- round your shoulders more.

(Susan does.)

And raise them up and down as if you're weeping.

(Susan does, to comic effect.)

Well, that doesn't seem right.

SUSAN. Well, is this it or not?

SALLIE. It's not how I would have you do it, but according to the diagram in the Shaftesbury manual…. this is grief.

SUSAN. Excellent. Next.

SALLIE. Wouldn't you rather be running lines?

SUSAN. We're doing the balcony today. I know the balcony. What I can't seem to remember are these gestures.

SALLIE. They'll come soon enough.

SUSAN. Not soon enough for Miss Cushman. And I'll be damned if I let that sister of mine get even a whiff of satisfaction over my failure. Next.

SALLIE. Let's see… Love.

SUSAN. Um…

(She makes a few false starts.)

SALLIE. This is Romeo and Juliet. You don't know "love"?

SUSAN. I know it, Sallie! Just… give me a moment. Um… wasn't it like…

(She puffs her chest and places her hand over her heart.)

CHARLOTTE. *(entering from the wings)* Wrong.

SUSAN. It is not. I've seen you do it.

CHARLOTTE. That's male love. Female love is like this…

(Manipulating Susan like a doll, Charlotte interlaces her fingers, places them under her chin, and tilts her head to the right.)

Now point your foot. The other one. There.

SUSAN. Well that's silly.

SALLIE. *(checking the book)* That's the posture.

SUSAN. No, I mean… men and women don't feel love differently.

CHARLOTTE. Of course we feel love differently. Our physiology is different, our minds.

SUSAN. Well it doesn't feel like that.

CHARLOTTE. Come Susan, we don't have time for--

SUSAN. No, Charlotte, you'll listen to me now. You may know more than me about the theatre, but love is one arena where I am the expert and you have no experience at all.

CHARLOTTE. *(Small pause. Then, smiling faintly:)* You're right. Tell me about men and women and love.

SUSAN. *(Now that she has the floor, she's uncertain how to say it.)* It's just that… when women love… it's more powerful than that. When we love it's… fearless. And that pose… it's weak. It's what men want us to be, not who we are.

CHARLOTTE. All right?

SUSAN. But you said… you said that we're trying to play the truth of love. Love more real than what men and women are permitted to perform in public. Right?

CHARLOTTE. Susie, I'm sure you have lots of big ideas in that pretty little head of yours, but--

SALLIE. *(to Charlotte)* Miss Cushman, hush. *(To Susan)* Go on, Miss Cushman.

SUSAN. What if we… what if we showed them the way love feels, instead of how it's supposed to look?

SALLIE. And how does it feel, Susan? To you.

SUSAN. It feels… like a tonic. A medicine.

CHARLOTTE. *(derisively)* Christ.

SALLIE. Shh!

SUSAN. It's stupid.

SALLIE. It's not.

SUSAN. I don't know how to say it right.

SALLIE. You do. Love feels like a tonic?

SUSAN. It gets inside you and… makes you better. Not like a beauty tonic or anything, although I do adore Madame Yale's Blood Tonic, my cheeks have never been rosier, and my hair–

CHARLOTTE. *(to Sallie)* Do you see?

SALLIE. *(to Susan)* Not a beauty tonic then. What's love's medicine?

SUSAN. I mean–just… it makes you stronger. Energized. Invincible. You can feel it coursing through you, powering you to be… more. Bigger. Love makes you as big as you've always been meant to be. You grow to meet the other person, to be all that they need.

SALLIE. *(moved)* That's… that's so lovely Susan. Who… who makes you feel that way?

CHARLOTTE. That's her private business–

SUSAN. Ned.

CHARLOTTE. Ned? I didn't even think you liked being a mother.

SUSAN. Oh, I don't. Being a mother is awful. But I love Ned so terribly I feel like my heart could burst.

CHARLOTTE. That makes no sense.

SUSAN. No. It doesn't.

(A pause.)

These gestures, these postures… they make us smaller. But that's not what love is.

CHARLOTTE. So what are you suggesting?

SUSAN. That we do the play without them.

CHARLOTTE. That's–absurd!

SALLIE. Actually it's not. Part of what audiences adore about you is that you're–untraditional. They find your spontaneity exciting.

SUSAN. Imagine how exciting Romeo and Juliet would feel if the lovers stopped doing what was expected of them?

CHARLOTTE. No gesture.

SALLIE. Just not the prescribed ones.

CHARLOTTE. You really think this could work?

(Sallie nods.)

It could be a disaster.

SALLIE. And it could be brilliant. Why don't we try it? We're rehearsing the balcony scene. Let's just see what it would be like. Throw away the blocking and let yourself… be big?

CHARLOTTE. Won't be a problem for me.

SALLIE. *(aside, to Charlotte, as Susan ascends the balcony)* You've got to give this a chance. She has… something.

CHARLOTTE. A presumptuous attitude is what she has.

SALLIE. Depth. She has depth. And instincts. She's not the empty-headed girl you've made her out to be.

CHARLOTTE. I wouldn't go that far.

SALLIE. She's a grown woman. A mother. And she's a Cushman. Make room for her to succeed. That's what you want, isn't it?

CHARLOTTE. I want this play to be ready by opening night.

SALLIE. Then I suppose you'll have to trust me, won't you?

SUSAN. *(from the balcony)* Where shall we take it from?

SALLIE. How about "good night"?

CHARLOTTE. Which one?

SALLIE. Right, right. The… the first one.

SUSAN. *(simply)* Good night, good night! as sweet repose and rest

Come to thy heart as that within my breast!

CHARLOTTE. *(grandly)* O, wilt thou leave me so unsatisfied?

SUSAN. What satisfaction canst thou have to-night?

CHARLOTTE. The exchange of thy love's faithful vow for
mine.

SALLIE. Wait. Miss Cushman.

CHARLOTTE & SUSAN. Which one?

SALLIE. Charlotte.

> *(A pause as the sisters take this in.)*

> It's not working.

CHARLOTTE. Well, I told you it wouldn't–

SALLIE. Because you aren't giving it a chance.

CHARLOTTE. Come on, I'm being natural. I'm not doing
the gestures.

SALLIE. But you may as well be.

CHARLOTTE. I don't follow.

SALLIE. It's still too much.

CHARLOTTE. I thought we were going for big.

SALLIE. I don't think big's the right way for you to go about
it.

CHARLOTTE. Well, there you go, Susan–

SALLIE. No. It's right for her. But not for you.

> *(She thinks for a moment.)*

> Juliet is "growing to meet" Romeo, as Susan said. What
if Romeo… makes room for that? Lets her love in?
Receives it.

CHARLOTTE. That sounds awfully feminine.

SALLIE. So?

CHARLOTTE. That's not what I do. Certainly not what
Romeo does.

SALLIE. Why not?

SUSAN. Sallie, it's all right, I don't know what I'm---

SALLIE. You're so powerful onstage. You're known for it.
What would thrill an audience more than seeing you

give some of that up? To see a Romeo who surrenders his power for love, makes himself vulnerable, loves bravely... like a woman?

CUSHMAN. This is nonsense. I've performed dozens of breeches roles–

SALLIE. Yes.

CHARLOTTE. –and the whole point is how I transform myself into a man.

SALLIE. Is it?

CHARLOTTE. No one wants to see a girlish Romeo. And no one wants to see me be girlish. God knows I failed at that my whole life.

SALLIE. All right, so forget whether they see you as a man or as a woman. Just be yourself. Don't try to play either. Just listen to Susan––really listen––then say Romeo's lines. And mean it.

(Charlotte looks to Susan uncomfortably.)

CHARLOTTE. This is the worst.

SALLIE. From "what satisfaction"?

CHARLOTTE. I hate you.

SALLIE. I hate you too. Whenever you're ready.

SUSAN. What satisfaction canst thou have to-night?

(Charlotte expands into Romeo, then stops. She looks to Sallie, who nods. She becomes Charlotte again.)

CHARLOTTE. The exchange of thy love's faithful vow for mine.

SALLIE. *(softly)* Good.

SUSAN. I gave thee mine before thou didst request it:
And yet I would it were to give again.

SALLIE. Now just say it.

CHARLOTTE. Wouldst thou withdraw it? for what purpose, love?

SUSAN. But to be frank, and give it thee again.

    And yet I wish but for the thing I have:

    My bounty is as boundless as the sea,

    My love as deep; the more I give to thee,

    The more I have, for both are infinite.

    (Charlotte takes this in–tears spring to her eyes, against her will. There is a moment between the sisters–recognition?)

SUSAN. Anon, good nurse! Sweet Montague, be true.

Stay but a little, I will come again.

CHARLOTTE. *(quiet, very vulnerable)* O blessed, blessed night! I am afeard

    Being in night, all this is but a dream,

    Too flattering-sweet to be substantial.

    (A pause. Very quiet.)

SUSAN. *(moved)* Charlotte….

CHARLOTTE. Don't.

SALLIE. It's GOOD, Miss Cushman.

CHARLOTTE. Don't patronize me. Either of you.

SUSAN. What do you mean? I–

CHARLOTTE. No one wants to see that. That's not what anyone is buying tickets for.

SALLIE. This is better.

SUSAN. If you would just trust us–

CHARLOTTE. Enough. This is my production. My name on the marquee. Enough fiddling around and indulging your amateurish ideas. Let's get this over with and then we'll never see each other again. Wasn't that the plan?

    (A silence. Then Matilda flies into the theatre with a box of pastries.)

MATILDA. Hello, hello, I hope I'm not interrupting. It's teatime, I thought... well, I was passing by and I thought, why don't I bring Miss Cushman and her compatriots something for tea?

(A pause.)

Is this a bad time?

SALLIE. Actually, Miss Hays–

MATILDA. I would just like a brief moment with Miss Cushman.

SUSAN. *(having come down from the balcony)* Hello, and who are you? Ooh, the little lemon cookies!

MATILDA. I'm–

CHARLOTTE. She's no one.

MATILDA. No one?!

CHARLOTTE. I mean… this is Miss Hays, of the English Ladies' Journal.

SUSAN. You didn't tell me there would be press today.

CHARLOTTE. You're right. I didn't. Excuse us for a moment. *(She takes Matilda aside. Hisses:)* I told you not to come here.

MATILDA. I know you did, darling. But I couldn't bear to leave things as they were. I'm sorry I was cross with you. *(even more quietly)* Please, my love.

CHARLOTTE. Keep your voice down.

MATILDA. Do you forgive me?

SALLIE. Miss Cushman? We really need to get back to work.

CHARLOTTE. *(to Sallie)* Yes.

MATILDA. Splendid! Then I'll stay.

CHARLOTTE. No!

SALLIE. We have three other scenes on the schedule today–

CHARLOTTE. *(yells)* One moment Sallie! *(whispers)* Max, I cannot have this conversation with you right now. I mean it. Go.

SUSAN. Charlotte, are you doing another interview?

CHARLOTTE. No. Miss Hays was just leaving.

MATILDA. You are the younger Miss Cushman, I assume?

SUSAN. I am. Susan.

MATILDA. A pleasure.

CHARLOTTE. All right, that's quite enough. This is a closed rehearsal, and my sister and I really must get back to work.

MATILDA. But–

SALLIE. Why don't you arrange for an interview with the theatre manager. Susan, let's start over, from the top?

SUSAN. *(ascending the balcony)* Lovely to meet you, Miss Hays! Thank you for the cookies!

MATILDA. *(as Charlotte hustles her towards the exit)* And you, Miss Cushman! *(to Charlotte)* She seems quite lovely! Why did you make her out to be such a dreadful cow?

CHARLOTTE. Max, are you out of your head? I explicitly told you that you and Susan were not to meet.

MATILDA. I don't see why I can't just–

(And the pair collide with a gussied-up Eleanora, who falls on her behind.)

ELEANORA. Oh! My dress! Charlotte, help me up!

MATILDA. "Charlotte"?

SALLIE. Miss Hays, why don't I introduce you to Mister Webster–

CHARLOTTE. *(hisses to Sallie)* Didn't you tell her not to-?!

SALLIE. I–forgot.

CHARLOTTE. I needed one thing. *(helping Eleanora up, quietly)* Now's not a good time, little one.

MATILDA. Who is this?

SALLIE. ONE THING?!

ELEANORA. But you said–

CHARLOTTE. *(to Matilda)* No one. *(to Sallie)* Wasting time with Susan instead of–

ELEANORA. –you said we could have another acting lesson today!

MATILDA. No one like I'm no one?

SALLIE. *(to Charlotte)* You leave EVERYTHING to me!

SUSAN. *(from the balcony)* Oh Romeo, Romeo–

CHARLOTTE. I never said–

SUSAN. Wherefore art thou Romeo?

ELEANORA. Why yes you did! When I left your dressing room after our last lesson, you told me, Eleanora, come by on Wednesday afternoon–

SUSAN. Deny thy father–

MATILDA. Your dressing room?

SUSAN. –and refuse thy name, or if thou wilt–

SALLIE. You wouldn't even be here if–

ELEANORA. *(pouting)* You promised me acting lessons!

SUSAN. *(annoyed)* Shall I go on?

MATILDA. *(Suddenly she knows.)* I see. Acting lessons.

CHARLOTTE. *(An admission.)* Max…

MATILDA. *(coldly, to Eleanora)* She gave me "acting lessons" once. Enjoy it while it lasts, dearie. She'll put you through your paces. But her lessons aren't worth the price. *(Holding back tears.)* I found that out the hard way. Goodbye, Miss Cushman.

(She leaves.)

ELEANORA. Price? But you said they'd be free!

SUSAN. Sallie? Charlotte? What is going on?

SALLIE. Take a break, Susan.

ELEANORA. Is this her? Your sister? *(whispers)* She's not as pretty as all that!

CHARLOTTE. Eleanora. Pet. Please. This is not a good time. Once we've opened the show, we may resume–

SUSAN. I don't want to take a break, I want to work.

CHARLOTTE. Now you want to work.

SALLIE. This isn't Susan's fault. Or mine.

ELEANORA. But it's not fair!

CHARLOTTE. *(seductively)* "That fair for which love groan'd for and would die, with tender Juliet match'd, is now not fair."

(Eleanora gives a little shiver.)

Come now, Nora. Give us just a bit more time and when you come with me to the provinces, the hard work will all be done. You'll just get to stand there, look lovely, get romanced by me every night, and be Juliet. You'd like that, wouldn't you?

ELEANORA. Oh, yes.

CHARLOTTE. Then run along now. I'll send for you later.

ELEANORA. Yes, Charlotte.

CHARLOTTE. That's a good girl.

SUSAN. Are we really taking a break?

SALLIE. Yes.

CHARLOTTE. No. Let's get back to work.

SALLIE. Sure you're not expecting any more visitors?

CHARLOTTE. Don't start. *(to Susan)* Let's start.

WEBSTER. *(bursting into the theatre with a newspaper)* We're doomed. It's all over. Stop the rehearsal.

CHARLOTTE. Or not.

ELEANORA. Shall I still go?

SALLIE. Mr. Webster! What do you mean? Why?

WEBSTER. Just look.

(He shows Sallie the paper. She blanches.)
You see?

SALLIE. Oh no.

CHARLOTTE. A scandal sheet? It can't be that bad.

SALLIE. It's bad.

WEBSTER. It's terrible.

ELEANORA. Which is it? Echoes of the Week? Town and Table? The Ladies' Column?

CHARLOTTE. Give it here.

(She scans the pages.)

Oh no.

SUSAN. What? What have you done now?

SALLIE. *(To Susan)* Miss Cushman–

SUSAN. Come on, out with it. You insult me, mock my ideas, then your friends interrupt our first productive rehearsal in weeks… what indignity have you brought upon our show, our family in the gossip columns?

SALLIE. Susan, don't.

SUSAN. I've had about enough of your superior attitude when it's you who––

WEBSTER. It's not.

SUSAN. What?

WEBSTER. It's not her. It's you.

(Charlotte crumples the paper, hiding it behind her back.)

SUSAN. No. Read it.

CHARLOTTE. Suzy.

SUSAN. Read it, I said.

(Charlotte and Sallie reluctantly exchange the paper.)

SALLIE. *(quietly)* "Rumors abound that the younger Miss Cushman, a single lady of twenty three, has an eight year old child, which would have made her a mother at the tender age of fourteen. The actresses' former beau is rumored to be Nelson Merriman, a man over fifty years her senior–"

CHARLOTTE. Enough!

SUSAN. *(to Charlotte)* Shut up and let her say it. *(to Sallie)* Go on.

SALLIE. "Between her youth and the distressing fact that the child's father is nowhere to be found, it begs the question of the legitimacy of the child's birth and moreover, the quality of Miss Cushman's moral character."

SUSAN. *(steely)* What else?

CHARLOTTE. That's all.

SUSAN. Liar. Your lip always twitches like that when you lie. Sallie.

SALLIE. "Can an English audience accept the mother of a bastard child as the virginal, pure heroine of Shakespeare's greatest love story? And what other scandalous acts might the younger Miss Cushman have committed that we've yet to discover?"

(A pause. Everyone looks at Susan.)

SUSAN. Well, that's it then. I'm ruined. Who will want me now?

CHARLOTTE. Susan…

SUSAN. Don't you dare, Charlotte. You brought me to this horrible town. And worse–you left me at home with a mother who didn't know how to take care of herself, let alone me. You left me alone to be married off to that lecherous old man, and look what it's done to me.

CHARLOTTE. I was only trying to–

SUSAN. I'm your sister when I'm useful to you and the rest of the time I can rot!

CHARLOTTE. We can fix this–

SUSAN. It doesn't matter now. I'll never show my face again.

(She bolts from the room, a single sob escaping her throat. Everyone watches her leave. A tense pause.)

ELEANORA. Does that mean I play Juliet this weekend?

(Charlotte and Sallie look at each other and run off together in the opposite direction. Webster and Eleanora are left alone.)

WEBSTER. Don't ask me. I just run the theatre. I never know what's going on.

SCENE 4

Edwin Forrest in his dressing room. He is large and imposing, his deep voice loud and full of bluster. A star and he knows it. He sits at his mirror, in profile, removing makeup and drinking from a flask. He is in a terrible mood. We hear a knock on his door.

FORREST. I said I was not to be disturbed.

> *(The knocks repeat.)*

Leave me alone, I say!

> *(Again, more insistent.)*

Are you deaf or just an idiot? No autographs. Go away!

> *(The door bursts open and in walk Charlotte and Sallie with a bouquet of pink and purple flowers and an armful of newspapers.)*

CHARLOTTE. Oh hello, Forrest. Don't mind us, this will be brief. Wouldn't want to delay you on your way to the bar.

FORREST. Cushman. I should have known.

CHARLOTTE. Sallie, could you please put those flowers in water?

FORREST. You can't seem to stay away from me, following me from city to city. If you weren't such a notorious prude I'd be terrified that you're in love with me.

CHARLOTTE. No one could rival you for your own

affections. And I had this engagement booked long before you made yours.

FORREST. Oh, you've been keeping track of my bookings have you?

CHARLOTTE. I can't help it if the British have a taste for American actors. Some of us, anyway. That was a rough audience.

FORREST. That was you hissing in the balcony. Of course it was.

CHARLOTTE. Oh no, I was down in the orchestra, quiet as a mouse.

FORREST. Good god, I hate the English.

SALLIE. Isn't your wife a Brit?

FORREST. Her most of all! These limey pricks wouldn't know good acting if it bit them on the ass.

CHARLOTTE. They might have enjoyed that more than they did your performance.

FORREST. What are you doing here, Cushman? Don't you have anything better to do? Or has your farce of a Romeo already been canceled?

CHARLOTTE. Oh no, Romeo and Juliet is still very much on. Despite your best efforts.

FORREST. I have no idea what you're talking about. *(snorts)* A woman playing Romeo. It's a joke. Nearly as ridiculous as your Hamlet.

CHARLOTTE. My ridiculous Hamlet was a success, unlike yours.

FORREST. Oh, shut up–

CHARLOTTE. Mine ran in Philadelphia for three more weeks than your production did–

FORREST. Mine was in a larger house!

CHARLOTTE. –and toured New England for another six–

FORREST. It was a side show!

CUSHMAN. –whereas yours was called… what was it? "Painfully unsubtle? Lacking psychological nuance? Like watching a gorilla try to enact the Bard?"

FORREST. A woman can never play the truth of manhood. Never. You're like a child playing dress up. It's an affront to real men.

(Sallie holds up a cloth covered in Forrest's brown stage makeup–maybe a cartoonish face-print?)

SALLIE. Your Othello was… interesting. I wonder how well you feel you can play the truth of a real moor.

FORREST. Your maid is mouthy.

CHARLOTTE. Sallie's not my maid. She's my assistant. And she may speak whenever she wishes.

FORREST. These limp-wristed English morons want someone to elocute. To speak pretty words, and gesture prettily, and prance about the stage. But that's not what The Moor is about. He's a man. He's about action. He's about sweat, and passion, and violence, and a hard cock. They're afraid of my virility. History will prove that my Othello is the definitive Othello. Meanwhile, the pretentious limey twats can all flock to your little peep show.

CHARLOTTE. Lovely job on the flowers, Sallie. They would look perfect on Mr. Forrest's dressing table. Would you…?

FORREST. "Breeches roles." Preposterous gimmick. Ladies in pants, letting audiences ogle your anatomy and pretending that it's about Shakespeare.

CHARLOTTE. I'm the biggest name in the Shakespearen theatre.

FORREST. You're an insult. The fact that anyone dares compare us – "the two great American actors in London" – insults me. I'm insulted by your grotesque pantomime of masculinity, and that anyone would put that on the same stages where I perform great roles. You're not even an actress, you're a novelty act. A freakshow. Don't kid yourself, Cushman. No one is coming to see your acting, they're coming to see your legs.

(Quickly and violently, Charlotte stomps one foot up onto Forrest's dressing table, baring one meaty leg and trapping Forrest at the table.)

CHARLOTTE. Do you think anyone would pay a nickel to see this leg? Kindly shut the fuck up, Forrest.

FORREST. Get that tree trunk out of my face.

CHARLOTTE. Your envy is transparent as it always has been.

FORREST. You have nothing I want, Cushman.

CHARLOTTE. Fine, I'll say it. You've hated me since Macbeth.

FORREST. My Macbeth was magnificent!

SALLIE. That's not what the critics wrote.

FORREST. The play is called Macbeth, not Lady Macbeth. It was my show! Mine! And you stole it from me!

CHARLOTTE. One stage isn't big enough for the both of us. Fine. I have no interest in playing opposite you again. I've seen what you do to your co-stars. You cut nearly all of poor Desdemona's lines–

FORREST. Everyone knows she's going to die. Just get on with it, I say.

CHARLOTTE. –and changed the whole script to ensure that you're always onstage. You don't care about these plays, only yourself. You're a ham. You're not actually a better actor than anyone else. You're just louder.

FORREST. *(loudly)* How dare you! I'm also taller.

CHARLOTTE. We'll never share the stage again. But we have to be able to work in the same city without these childish hijinks.

FORREST. I don't know what you're referring to.

SALLIE. We know it was you, Mr. Forrest. Who ran to the papers maligning the younger Miss Cushman.

FORREST. Such an unfortunate situation. A reckless, promiscuous woman, a bastard child, rumors of whoring… But unfortunately for you, I'm not the one who shared your poor sister's shameful past with the press.

CHARLOTTE. Well, not to worry. We've taken care of it.

(She dumps a pile of newspapers on the dressing table.) I've had corrections printed.

FORREST. What?

SALLIE. Susan's marriage and divorce decrees. Ned's birth certificate, with his father's name on it.

CHARLOTTE. And the papers were happy to run a nice, long, juicy feature on Romeo and Juliet, star vehicle for the dynamic Cushman sisters.

SALLIE. The Haymarket says we're probably going to have to extend before we tour the provinces, with all the good press.

(Forrest quietly seethes.)

CHARLOTTE. You can't touch me, Forrest. I haven't nearly reached the height of my fame. I can feel it in my bones. They love me in Europe. They say I'm the best American actor the world has ever seen.

SALLIE. The only American actor capable of doing Shakespeare justice.

CHARLOTTE. And that has nothing to do with my legs. I'm on my way up.

SALLIE. And you're on your way out.

CHARLOTTE. The English have seen through you, realized that you're nothing but a loud voice and a big body, with no soul or brains inside.

SALLIE. And you can't seem to bribe the British press to puff up your performances the way you could American critics, can you?

FORREST. Of all the filthy, slanderous–

CHARLOTTE. Now Sallie, you know that Forrest's manager made those payments, not him. Isn't that right, Forrest?

FORREST. Piss off, Cushman. I'm done with you.

SALLIE. And your desperation has you resorting to such cheap tricks. That umber you wear is more of a gimmick than her breeches are. Perhaps leave the Moors to Ira Aldridge?

FORREST. I won't be spoken to like this by a presumptuous stagehand, much less a negress. What do you know about acting? About anything? Mind your place, girl.

CHARLOTTE. Her place is beside me. Sallie has been my dresser for many years.

FORREST. Stagehand, dresser. Who cares. A negro is a negro.

SALLIE. Was that your approach to Othello, or–?

CHARLOTTE. Aren't you tired of all this, Forrest? We needn't be in competition. The world is large enough for us both, provided we each stay out of the other's way. Why not leave each other be, quit the petty games, and conserve our energies for conquering the British stage. Each of us to our own. Truce?

(She extends her hand for Forrest, who looks at it disdainfully.)

FORREST. Nothing is ever enough for you women. First you want to go on the stage. Ridiculous, immodest, arrogant sluts–

CHARLOTTE. Now you're just sweet-talking me.

FORREST. –and we let you. We let you! And instead of being grateful, appreciating that we've indulged your little whims, you want to play the men's parts too! Women like you take, and take, and take and then spit in our faces and ask for more. Men invented the theatre. Refined it over centuries, created every great work in existence. We've earned our place. You don't deserve to just take it from us because you're suddenly fashionable. You won't be happy until you've taken everything from men. Well, I'm not going to roll over and swallow it, Cushman. I'm going to fight to keep what's mine.

(A pause.)

CHARLOTTE. Do you like the flowers, Mr. Forrest?

FORREST. Oh, shut up about the goddamned flowers.

CHARLOTTE. Being women, we've had to learn all kinds of things while you men were out building the culture all on your own. Frivolous things like embroidery, and knitting, learning to play an instrument. Do you know anything about floriography?

FORREST. Is there a point to this droning?

CHARLOTTE. *(fluffing the pink and purple flowers, and centering them on Forrest's dressing table)* The Language of Flowers. Secret messages sent through bouquets. Codes--each bloom has a distinct meaning, put them together and you can puzzle out the sentiment. My sister and I learned when we were young. These are monkshood, and woodbine. Perhaps you'd like to consult Shoberl's guide.

FORREST. I have more important things to do.

CHARLOTTE. Quite right. It seems like you need to go back to rehearsal if you'd like to continue selling tickets to this dud.

FORREST. Begone, harpy. You've had your fun.

CHARLOTTE. Good luck with what's left of Othello, Edwin.

SALLIE. A quick bit of advice: restore Desdemona's lines in four two. The play needs them. I promise you'll be alright if you stop talking for a page or two.

FORREST. Out!

CHARLOTTE. Enjoy the monkshood.

(They leave.)

FORREST. *(raging, possibly breaking something)*
Would I could thrash this loathsome, mannish shrew
As any other foe. I hate the Wom'n.
The English laud her gifts, her thund'rous voice;
Amer'can brashness, newness, strength and size;
yet I, my actor's charm and gifts the same,
With boos and hisses am I met withal.
My scheme to crush the younger, pretty thing
She's brought to woo the crowd has crashed and burned;
I'm thwarted by a simple document!
I must extinguish Cushman's damned light.
I—I must—she—I'll–
GOD–DAMNED–BITCHES! RAAAAAAHHHHH!
(He storms around the room, throwing a tantrum. He's about to break the vase of flowers, but stops, looking at it.)

MATILDA. *(entering, knocking softly against the open door frame)* Mister Forrest?

FORREST. Christ, another one. Out, out, out!

MATILDA. Excuse me, sir. I don't mean to disturb you. I'm Miss Hays, of the English Ladies' Journal.

FORREST. Call on the theatre manager if you want an interview.

MATILDA. No, this isn't about an interview–

FORREST.I don't have time for you or for the English Ladies' Journal. Get out of my dressing room and leave me in peace. Go. Now. Goodbye.

MATILDA. I want to help you destroy Charlotte Cushman's career.

FORREST. Hello.

MATILDA. Hello.

(A pause.)

You went after her sister.

FORREST. I did nothing of the sort!

MATILDA. That was a mistake. Susan's past may look sordid, but her marriage and her child were both legitimate. She's a fool, but she's not a prostitute.

FORREST. All actresses are prostitutes.

MATILDA. So then no one will care if she is, too. You're working the wrong angle.

FORREST. How's that?

MATILDA. You're not going to be able to shut Romeo and Juliet down based on Susan's sexual impropriety. You're going to have to do it based on Charlotte's.

FORREST. *(bursts out laughing)* I thought you were a journalist. Everyone knows that Charlotte Cushman may as well be a nun. That old spinster is going to die a virgin. Never having known the touch of a man.

MATILDA. You're right. She's never been with a man.

FORREST. So what are you going on about?

MATILDA. But she's no nun.

FORREST. I don't understand.

MATILDA. She–loves women.

FORREST. I don't see how her coterie of homely old maids are going to help me ruin her.

MATILDA. She loves women–the way other women love

men.

FORREST. *(very confused)* She...?

MATILDA. She makes love with women. *(bitterly)* Lots and lots of women.

FORREST. I don't understand. Two women... can't... How would they...? Everyone knows that women don't have carnal desires, as men do–

MATILDA. Believe me, they do. She does.

FORREST. *(as if he's trying to solve a particularly difficult math equation)* But... without a man, they couldn't...

MATILDA. Trust me, Forrest. She. Loves. Other. Women. Unnaturally.

FORREST. How do you know?

MATILDA. I have letters that can prove it.

(She produces them.)

I've blacked out the other woman's name. For her protection.

(Forrest looks them over, understanding dawning slowly.)

FORREST. "My passion for you... the deepest of loves... your caress" My god. She really is a freakshow!

(Matilda winces, but says nothing.)

We must have these published. Tomorrow!

MATILDA. I wouldn't.

FORREST. What do you mean? These letters are gold! Everything we need to shut down her little show and ruin her for good.

MATILDA. If you publish these letters now, you've played your entire hand. Better to publish something that lets her know you have them–that hints at it–and force her to cancel on her own.

FORREST. I see...

MATILDA. Then you have them in your back pocket, waiting, for the next time she tries to perform in the same city as you.

FORREST. Ha!

MATILDA. Or play a role you fancy playing. You can make her do whatever you want.

FORREST. Quite right.

(A pause.)

Who are you? Why do you want Cushman exposed, her career ruined?

MATILDA. Because she lied to me. Betrayed me. Made a fool of me. Because she's a self-involved, manipulative-

(She stops herself. Regains her composure.)

Because she deserves it.

FORREST. What was your name again? Miss…?

MATILDA. Hays.

FORREST. Miss Hays. You are an angel from heaven. Thank you. You can write this exposé? Get it in the papers?

MATILDA. I can. It can run tomorrow morning.

FORREST. And what do you want from me?

MATILDA. I want to go onstage again.

FORREST. Another great actress?

MATILDA. No, I'm not very good.

FORREST. Well that's–refreshing.

(He takes her chin in his hand. Turns her face this way and that.)

Fine, you'll do. Our Emilia keeps upstaging me in the final scene, screaming her damn head off, rending her garments and weeping. I need someone who won't pull focus. You can follow orders? And do as you're told?

MATILDA. Yes.

FORREST. See the manager and get your pages. You'll replace her once Cushman's Romeo is dead.

MATILDA. Thank you.

(She notices the vase of flowers on the dressing table.) Where did you get these?

FORREST. Cushman and her maid left them here. Some kind of joke.

MATILDA. These aren't a joke. These are a threat.

FORREST. What do you mean?

MATILDA. Woodbine. That's fraternal love. Or sisterly love, if you'd rather. And Monkshood – "beware a deadly foe".

FORREST. I don't…

MATILDA. Floriographically speaking, this bouquet means "hurt my sister and I'll kill you."

FORREST. Flowers can say that?

MATILDA. These do.

FORREST. Well. Better leave the sister out of it then.

(He extends his hand. Matilda takes it, and they shake on it.)

SCENE 5

*Sallie and Susan in the theatre, running lines.
Sallie holds a prompt book. Susan paces.*

SUSAN. *(with speed but understanding – it's clear she's
worked since last time.)*
Now, good sweet nurse–O Lord, why look'st thou sad?
Though news be sad, yet tell them merrily;
If good, thou shamest the music of sweet news
By playing it to me with so sour a face.

SALLIE. *(flatly–she's not an actress)* I am a-weary, give me
leave awhile:
Fie, how my bones ache! what a jaunt have I!

SUSAN. I would thou hadst my bones, and I thy news:
Nay, come, I pray thee, speak!
(Sallie waits.)
I said it right!
(Pause.)
Didn't I?

SALLIE. Almost. There's a bit more at the end. "Good, good
nurse…"

SUSAN. Damn! We perform tomorrow, we have to make up
for that entire lost day, and Charlotte will be here…
when?

SALLIE. Within the hour.

SUSAN. …and she'll be rested and ready to eviscerate me for a single missed syllable. Um… Nay come, I pray thee, speak. Good, good nurse, speak!

SALLIE. Jesu, what haste? can you not stay awhile?

Do you not see that I am out of breath?

SUSAN. *(double speed)* How art thou out of breath, when thou hast breath

To say to me that thou art out of breath?

The excuse that thou dost make in this delay

Is longer than the tale thou dost excuse.

Is thy news good, or bad? answer to that;

Say either, and I'll stay the circumstance:

Let me be satisfied, is't good or bad?

(Sallie smiles.)

Did I miss something?

SALLIE. No, I just–you're a lot like her, do you know that?

SUSAN. Juliet?

SALLIE. Your sister.

SUSAN. *(snorts)* Better not let her hear you say that. She's made it perfectly clear that she thinks I'm a shallow, prattling nobody. And she–well, she's Our Charlotte, no surname needed.

SALLIE. *(laughing)* God, those Boston headlines! I thought she had a big head before…

SUSAN. Oh, I can imagine she was thoroughly insufferable once "Cushmania" took hold. Not that I've seen much of her since then.

SALLIE. Well, we've been very busy.

SUSAN. She's all anyone wanted to talk to me about–Our Charlotte, the biggest star in the sky, wasn't it exciting, and wasn't I lucky to be her sister. As if some of her glory might pass to them through me. Silly.

(A pause. She clears her throat.)

We're nothing alike, really. That's why we fight all the time.

SALLIE. I'd argue that it's the opposite.

SUSAN. Come on, let's run more lines. I want to be ready for tomorrow.

SALLIE. You've rehearsed your scenes to death.

SUSAN. What about the Friar Lawrence scene?

SALLIE. Miss Cushman–you're ready.

(Susan releases a tense breath.)

You care about this, don't you. You're not just trying to get it over with, or placate your sister. You want to be good.

SUSAN. No. I don't want to be laughed at, that's all. I want to leave this awful, damp city with some dignity.

SALLIE. I think you'll leave with more than that.

SUSAN. Thank you, Miss Mercer.

(A pause.)

Thank you for the other day, too.

SALLIE. For…?

SUSAN. The balcony scene. You listened to me. Got her to try it my way, even though she didn't want to. How did you do that?

SALLIE. Your sister and I have an understanding.

SUSAN. She must care for you a great deal.

SALLIE. And I her.

SUSAN. Is that the reason behind your loyalty? You're a free woman, you could do anything.

(Sallie shoots her a pointed look.)

Well, nearly. Why are you content being my sister's dresser all these years?

SALLIE. It's partly our friendship, yes. She pays me very

well, enough to live better than most, and send something home to my family. I get to travel the world, meet important people. And I get to be near the plays.

SUSAN. Near them?

SALLIE. To hear them, think about them. Bring them to life as they're meant to be.

SUSAN. I don't understand.

SALLIE. My mother made sure I could read, said it could be a matter of survival. So as a girl, she'd give me books, as many as I wanted, and I would read them, to the exclusion of everything else.

SUSAN. That sounds lonely.

SALLIE. On the contrary. I loved to be inside the stories, to disappear into the lives of Elizabeth Bennet and Don Quixote, even Doctor Frankenstein. That losing myself– it was ecstatic. And then I found the plays. Shakespeare's. And I read them all. Then I read them again. And as I read, I could see them, so clearly in my head, more than any other worlds I'd visited in any other books. And one day when I was fourteen, I saved up enough money to go see Charlotte in Twelfth Night when it came to Philadelphia. I was so excited it was unbearable. I was shaking, waiting for the curtain to rise. I had waited all my life to see these plays on stage, to see them how they were in my head, and it was… wrong. All wrong. It wasn't at all as I'd imagined it.

SUSAN. Oh no!

SALLIE. So I waited for her outside the theatre, and I accosted her the moment she walked out and gave her a piece of my mind for ruining the play.

SUSAN. *(aghast)* She must have been furious!

SALLE. She was… intrigued, maybe? That I had the nerve to say such things, or just that anyone would criticize her at all. We stood outside the theatre for an hour and

I tried to make her see what I saw, how I had imagined Viola and the play. The sweet sadness of it, that it wasn't only a comedy about a girl dressed as a boy, but a story of longing and loss, and the joy that only comes after sorrow. I made her see it as I did, told her that the play needed to be so much more than it was that night, and that she had to change it. That the play deserved it.

SUSAN. Did she excoriate you?!

SALLIE. Far from it.

SUSAN. She hired you as her dresser.

SALLIE. Yes. And while I assisted her, we talked. I'd tell her how to adjust a certain scene, or line. I'd see something she didn't, and we'd argue and then I'd watch her understand. And as we worked together, she transformed. She became Our Charlotte. I see the Shakespeare of my imagination, made real in her performances. My ideas, onstage in front of an audience, and no one knows they're mine. I'm invisible and somehow on the stage at once. It's the greatest thrill of my life.

SUSAN. You wouldn't want to perform yourself?

SALLIE. I shouldn't like the attention; I don't enjoy being looked at. And I'd much rather be the brains behind the most famous actress in the world than cope with fame myself. I'm happy in the wings. Anonymous.

SUSAN. Well, I'm glad you're content, I suppose. To me it just sounds like more of the same: Charlotte makes use of us to polish her own image, and then when she's done, she leaves us in the dust.

SALLIE. Your metaphor needs work.

SUSAN. You know what I mean.

SALLIE. Hasn't your sister been sending money to you all this time? Set aside savings for your son's future?

SUSAN. Paying us off to leave her alone.

SALLIE. You really believe that?

(An uncomfortable silence.)

Do you even know what she did for you? When they published those things in the paper about you and Ned?

SUSAN. I know she released those documents so my shame wouldn't sully her good name.

SALLIE. Not that. When she went to Mr. Forrest.

(A pause.)

She didn't tell you. Your sister went to the man she despises most in the world and made a peace offering on your behalf.

SUSAN. *(uncertainly)* That doesn't sound like Charlotte.

SALLIE. And when he denied her, she threatened him with severe bodily harm if he dared interfere with you again.

SUSAN. That does.

SALLIE. Think what you want about Miss Cushman, but she would do anything for you. She was willing to humble herself before Edwin Forrest, of all people, in order to restore your honor.

SUSAN. And in the next moment she was only too willing to, what, challenge him to a duel?

SALLIE. When he insulted you, yes. You should have seen the look in her eye. I've only seen it once before, when she had a fencing foil in her hand in the final scene of Hamlet. You'll never have a more fearsome protector.

SUSAN. What I wish I had was a normal sister.

SALLIE. Why would you want that?

(A pause.)

SUSAN. Let's run the lines for three-two again. Just one more time.

SALLIE. As you like, Miss.

SUSAN. Gallop apace, you fiery-footed steeds,

Towards Phoebus' lodging: such a wagoner

As Phaethon would–

(As before, Webster bursts into the theatre with a newspaper.)

WEBSTER. That's it, this time we're well and truly buggered. My apologies, ladies, but–shit! Shit! Shit!

SALLIE. Mister Webster!

SUSAN. What now? My physician's records? My grade-school marks?

WEBSTER. *(to Sallie)* Did you know about this?

SALLIE. About WHAT?

WEBSTER. Of course you did. You know everything! I should have known better than to let myself be run around by a pack of women. The Haymarket is sunk! And me with it!

SALLIE. I suggest that you don't point your finger at me, sir.

WEBSTER. So polite! And all the while you've been dragging me into this–this–den of iniquity!

SUSAN. I haven't done anything wrong! It's been proven! Haven't you seen the retractions?

WEBSTER. A Lady Romeo!, they said! A great idea! You'll sell out every show! Your theatre will be in the black for years! Bollocks!

SALLIE. Mister Webster! I suggest that you regain your composure at once and tell us what the matter is. Really. I thought Englishmen had more dignity than this!

WEBSTER. You're right. I'm sorry Miss. I– *(he begins laughing)* Just when I thought I'd seen it all.

(He stuffs the paper in Sallie's hands and begins to leave.)

She's your problem now, ladies.

SUSAN. Where are you going?

WEBSTER. To find some gin.

(He's gone.)

SUSAN. *(as Sallie searches the paper)* It can't be!

SALLIE. Oh no.

SUSAN. You said–you said it had all been settled. That Charlotte had fixed it. How can they still–I was married! At fourteen! And then left alone with my child!

SALLIE. Oh god.

SUSAN. How can anyone blame me for that? How–

SALLIE. Susan.

SUSAN. But it's not right!

SALLIE. It's not about you.

SUSAN. *(snatching the paper)* Then what– "by Miss Matilda Hays"? Wasn't that Charlotte's friend, with the cookies?

(She stops, squints at the paper. Gasps, then laughs.)

SALLIE. *(gravely)* Susan.

SUSAN. Surely this can't mean…

SALLIE. That's exactly what it means.

SUSAN. *(The color drains from her face as she reads further.)* Oh, good god in heaven. What are we going to do?

(Just then, Charlotte enters, in full Romeo costume and high spirits.)

CHARLOTTE. Final dress rehearsal! I hope you're both as excited as I am. Sallie, would you please make sure that all the props are in their proper place–I had no poison last night and had to stab myself instead, can't repeat that fiasco. Set an extra one up left, if you would? The rest of the company arrives in an hour. Susan, that gives us just enough time to run our scenes together. I think–

Suzie, I think we're going to be marvelous.
(They stare at her.)
What?

END ACT I

INTERMISSION

ACT II

SCENE 1

Charlotte and Webster enter, mid-argument. Webster's arms are filled with playbills, along with a bottle of gin, which he's already started drinking.

CHARLOTTE. –it's foul gossip, nothing more!

WEBSTER. It is that.

CHARLOTTE. Just give me a day to get it cleared up. We'll have retractions printed, just as we did for Susan!

WEBSTER. I'm afraid, Miss Cushman, that this is far too grave an accusation for the Haymarket to continue your engagement. We are canceling. Immediately. Before we lose any more money on this fiasco.

CHARLOTTE. But it isn't true!

WEBSTER. It doesn't matter if it's true. No one in London will buy tickets to your play. And if we don't cancel, they may not buy tickets to any more plays here again. We can't be associated–

CHARLOTTE. Coward!

WEBSTER. –with this kind of degeneracy, true or not–

CHARLOTTE. –but we open tomorrow night!

WEBSTER. *(raising his voice)* Not any longer, you don't!

(Charlotte is taken aback.)

Since the moment you arrived here, you've done nothing but strut and bully and throw your weight around. Typical American!

CHARLOTTE. How dare you! You should count yourself lucky to–

WEBSTER. Enough. Bombast won't work on me anymore. Nor anyone else in London, I should think. Your reputation is going in the bin, along with these playbills. You're through here.

CHARLOTTE. We'll see about that! I can take Romeo to any other stage in town–

WEBSTER. You can't. *(his voice softens)* I take no pleasure in this, Miss Cushman. Truly I don't. It's just business. Pounds and pence. It might be best for you to return to America. See your family. Enjoy a hiatus.

(Charlotte slumps. She knows he's right.)

You know, I've had quite a storied career myself, Miss Cushman. I've performed on this very stage hundreds of times. Maybe thousands. Well, I used to, anyway. Before I was elevated to manager, and it stopped being any fun. I was funny, did you know that? Funniest actor in London, they said. I had them rolling in the aisles six nights a week. But now it's just pounds and pence. Twenty years managing the Haymarket and now I'm lucky to get onstage once a year.

CHARLOTTE. Well, that won't be me.

WEBSTER. You're right. When this story follows you home, you won't be allowed anywhere near a theatre ever again, onstage or off.

CHARLOTTE. You're going to regret this, Webster.

(Webster takes a big swig from the bottle of gin.)

WEBSTER. On that, Miss Cushman, we agree. Luckily… I'm used to regrets. In the meantime… Take my advice and leave London. For good.

(Webster takes another swig and shuffles off the stage. Charlotte is alone.)

CHARLOTTE. Ha, banishment! be merciful, say 'death'.
    My empire, fame, the walls that I have built
    Now crumble down around me into dust.
    They know. And now, I will be punished for…
    What? My crime to love? My crime to lie.
    My crime to hide my secrets in plain sight.
    I was adored once; that's all finished now.
    My public's love will loathing soon become,
    And Susan will renounce me as her kin,
    My little lover's ardor shall dissolve;
    So Sallie too shall purge me from her life.
    No hope. No future. Nothing left to do.
    Matilda's vengeance for my callousness
    Here ends 'Cushmania'. I am undone.
    (She picks up a stray playbill, looks at it for a moment, and crumples it.)
    Goddamn it.

SUSAN. *(appearing at the balcony)* Is it really over?

CHARLOTTE. Where's Sallie?

SUSAN. Cleaning out the dressing rooms. You can fight this, you know. It's libelous. Hideous. That Miss Hays would spread such lies–

CHARLOTTE. Get out, Susan.

SUSAN. Rumors like this are terrible, but they fade. You should have heard the way people talked in Boston when I married Nelson–

CHARLOTTE. You don't know anything. Send Sallie in.

SUSAN. You're right, I don't know anything! Because you never tell me!

CHARLOTTE. Go home.

SUSAN. This again? You're going to send me away, leave me behind? Back on the shelf until I'm a convenient prop again?

CHARLOTTE. I've done nothing but care for you your whole pampered life!

SUSAN. Care for me? You've gone years without visiting. I once had to read in the paper that you were coming to Boston, and sit in the audience to see you at all!

CHARLOTTE. Oh for–

SUSAN. When I was carrying Ned and that horrible old man abandoned me, just as father abandoned us as girls–

CHARLOTTE. How is any of that my fault?!

SUSAN. –you didn't come to see me. Not once. I was all alone.

CHARLOTTE. Because I was working twice as much so I could send you more money! Are you really that stupid?

SUSAN. I didn't need money. I needed my sister!

CHARLOTTE. Oh, you didn't need the money? You certainly spent it!

SUSAN. Don't you dare throw that in my face.

CHARLOTTE. All I've ever been to you is a bank. And you were always happy to collect, weren't you?

(Susan is quiet.)

Well, time to find another hustle. The bank is closing. Charlotte Cushman is done.

SUSAN. Done with what?

(Pause.)

Charlotte.

CHARLOTTE. I. Want. Sallie.

SUSAN. You can talk to me!

CHARLOTTE. Since when?

SUSAN. I don't understand! Why don't you fight?

CHARLOTTE. Why don't you mind your business?

SUSAN. You made this my business when you brought me here. When you put me onstage, when you made me play Juliet!

CHARLOTTE. Well you've finally gotten what you wanted. You're free of Juliet, free of the play, and free of me.

SUSAN. I want to do the play, Charlotte. I need to.

CHARLOTTE. Then you had better go and get yourself another Romeo. I'm box office poison. No stage in London will have me.

SUSAN. I can't do it without you. I won't.

CHARLOTTE. What about this aren't you understanding? It's over for me. I can't beat this.

SUSAN. How can you say that? How is this any different from–

CHARLOTTE. It's completely different!

SUSAN. It's just more gossip! You can–

CHARLOTTE. I can't!

SUSAN. But why?

CHARLOTTE. Because Matilda has my goddamned letters!

SUSAN. Matilda–has–you mean what she wrote in the paper… is… true?

CHARLOTTE. ....

SUSAN. You… with other ladies?

CHARLOTTE. *(numbly)* Now will you leave?

SUSAN. I never knew.

(Susan awkwardly sits next to Charlotte.)

But, are you sure? How does it even… work, without a man?

CHARLOTTE. *(jumping up)* Fine, I'll leave.

SUSAN. No, wait! Please. I'm sorry. Just… let me catch up.

(They look at each other from opposite sides of the bare stage. Charlotte isn't going to speak, so Susan must.)
The other day… the balcony. Something happened. You let me see you. You, as I remembered you before you left home, before you became Our Charlotte. I hadn't seen that person since I was a girl. I've missed her.

CHARLOTTE. You don't know me.

SUSAN. I'd like to.

CHARLOTTE. Why?

SUSAN. Because we're sisters!

CHARLOTTE. You say that as if it means something! As if something as arbitrary as blood could bind us together, could allow you to see me as I am, as I truly am, and not turn away from me!

SUSAN. So show me.

(Charlotte stiffens, but stays.)
You should come home. To Boston. There's room for you at the house.

CHARLOTTE. I can't think of anything more wretched.

SUSAN. Thanks.

CHARLOTTE. Besides, Forrest will come back to America soon, and it will start all over again. Even if I'm not acting anymore, he'll see that the truth gets out. That this follows me wherever I go. Better for me to disappear.

SUSAN. And never act again.

CHARLOTTE. Only in the role I'm worst at: "Lady".

SUSAN. There has to be another way.

CHARLOTTE. There's not. It's best for you and mother if I don't come home. You can tell her that I fell ill. I'll keep sending money for as long as I can, and when it stops, she'll just believe that I succumbed.

SUSAN. You can't possibly think that mother would prefer

you were dead than–

CHARLOTTE. Than a lover of women? Wake up, Susan.

SUSAN. Please, if you'll just let me help you–

CHARLOTTE. Stop pretending as if you could bear treating me as your sister when I'm not famous anymore, when I'm not wealthy, when I'm just a liability–

SUSAN. You are my sister–

CHARLOTTE. You won't have me anywhere near you, embarrassing you and ruining your prospects.

SUSAN. Is that what you think of me?

CHARLOTTE. I think you're a shallow, selfish, spoiled baby. You always have been, and you always will be.

SUSAN. *(stung)* You don't mean that.

CHARLOTTE. Take my advice: find a new Romeo.

SUSAN. I would never–

CHARLOTTE. Or just quit and get married again! I don't care what you do. As long as you forget that I exist.

SUSAN. I'm not the one you're angry at. Not this time. You know that I–

CHARLOTTE. I know who you really are. You've fooled Sallie by playing at being a grown up, at caring about the play, about me. But I know better. I feel sorry for Ned, to have a mother who can't love anything but herself.

(A terrible pause. Charlotte has gone too far.)

SUSAN. *(steely)* You're right, Charlotte. I don't know you at all. And you certainly don't know me.

(She storms off.)

SCENE 2

Forrest's dressing room. Matilda paces, waiting. She seems anxious, and as if she's been waiting for some time.

MATILDA. *(muttering to herself)* It serves her right. It serves her right.

(She startles, leaping up as footsteps approach)

FORREST. *(from off)* "Exchange me for a goat before I turn the business of my soul to just exsufflicate and blowed surmises–"

(entering) Jesus Christ! What are you doing here?

MATILDA. It's been canceled. The Romeo and Juliet. Last night.

FORREST. Right. Well done. So?

MATILDA. So, we were supposed to meet today? To put me in as Emilia?

FORREST. Oh, were we?

MATILDA. Yes. Three hours ago.

FORREST. Damndest thing, apparently the manager is rather attached to the scenery-chewer. He says we can't replace her.

MATILDA. But–you said that if Charlotte canceled–then I'd–

FORREST. Next time, Miss Hays. Next time.

MATILDA. I don't understand. We made a bargain. I

released a gossip item that closed Charlotte Cushman's play. I held up my end. Now it's time for you to make good on yours.

FORREST. Alas, Miss Hays, the theatre is a fickle mistress. And some promises simply can't be kept.

MATILDA. Then it's not a promise.

FORREST. Don't be so dreary. We've won, the amazon has lost. We should celebrate! Brandy?

MATILDA. This early in the day?

FORREST. Special occasion.

MATILDA. Well… all right.

> *(She sips. Forrest watches her.)*

Oh, I almost forgot to tell you. There's a letter for you, on your dressing table. The manager said it was left at the stage door early this morning.

FORREST. Ah, fan mail! It does get tiresome. But that's the price of stardom.

MATILDA. There's also the matter of my letters.

FORREST. What's that?

MATILDA. Or, Miss Cushman's. The ones I brought here yesterday? You kept them to review. I should like to have them back.

FORREST. Oh, I'm afraid I can't do that either. More brandy?

MATILDA. I must insist that you return my letters!

FORREST. *(opening his 'fan mail')* Here's the thing, Miss Hays. I couldn't figure out why, exactly, you wanted to delay the publication of these sapphic missives–

MATILDA. I told you yesterday–

FORREST. Hang them over her head, yes. Let them control her without completely destroying her. But then I got to thinking–

MATILDA. Did you.

FORREST. –why wait? I want to be rid of her. Permanently. And these letters are a killing blow.

MATILDA. Mister Forrest, with all due respect–

FORREST. So I contacted my friend at the Illustrated London News and arranged to have them published in tonight's evening press.

MATILDA. But we agreed that it would be best–

FORREST. Don't worry, I won't reveal who the letters are written to. As long as you don't cross me.

MATILDA. *(starts, quietly)* What?

FORREST. You English think you're so much smarter than us big dumb Americans. You thought you could come here, into my dressing room, and manipulate me, get everything you wanted–a role in my play, a little control over Charlotte Cushman, and that I'd be too stupid to catch on. You thought wrong. I know what you are.

MATILDA. What I– you– you are quite mistaken.

FORREST. Oh, I think not. Now, if you value your own reputation, Miss Hays, I'd make a point of staying out of my way. Don't come here again, don't ask for anything from me, don't mention me to anyone. I don't want to see my name anywhere near your byline. I'll make an exception for a glowing review, of course.

MATILDA. Those letters belong to me. I demand that you give them back–at once.

FORREST. Or what?

(He advances and looms over her menacingly–clearly much larger than she is. He takes her brandy glass.)

Females have forgotten the natural order of things. We let you write in our papers, and perform on our stages, even study at our universities, and you think that makes you equal. But in any real confrontation–a match of wits, or of stamina, of grit, of character or physical strength–it's obvious who's the dominant sex. Who's in charge. Go on making believe you're equal, Miss Hays. But don't be surprised if it gets you into trouble.

MATILDA. *(meekly)* Whatever it is you imagine you know about me–you're wrong.

FORREST. *(unfolding the letter)* Whatever you need to tell yourself.

(Reading, he begins to laugh.)

Oh, this is quite a development.

MATILDA. You're every bit as despicable as Charlotte said you were.

FORREST. –even better than I could have ever dreamed!

MATILDA. What? Your fan mail?

FORREST. Not quite. "Dear Mister Forrest, due to recent revelations--"

(Susan appears, not in the room.)

SUSAN. –and out of concern for my own reputation, my future, and my immortal soul, I have made the decision to separate myself from my sister. I would like to ally myself professionally with

SUSAN & FORREST. the most gifted American actor in London

FORREST. "and remount Romeo and Juliet with you!"

MATILDA. No!

SUSAN. If this agrees with you, I shall be very pleased. I will call today at midday to discuss the possibility of our partnership.

SUSAN & FORREST. "Kindly, Miss Susan Cushman."

(Susan vanishes.)

MATILDA. How could she?

FORREST. Everyone's out for themselves, Miss Hays. I'll

give you that bit of show business advice for free. Now get out of my dressing room. I have a lunch date.

MATILDA. You're right to hate Charlotte. She's arrogant, and vain, and self-important. But she's a better actor than you will ever be. You'll have to live with knowing that, even if she never performs again.

FORREST. Pip pip, cheerio, Miss Hays. Don't let the door hit your ass on the way out.

(Matilda opens the door to leave. On the other side of it stands Susan.)

SUSAN. So sorry for the late notice. I hope it's alright that I came.

FORREST. Miss Cushman. Of course it is. Welcome, do sit down. Miss Hays was just leaving. Weren't you, Miss Hays?

(Matilda looks from Susan to Forrest anxiously, opens her mouth to speak, then closes it.)

MATILDA. Quite right. Goodbye, Mr. Forrest. Miss Cushman.

(And she leaves.)

FORREST. Well. "Beauty too rich for use, for earth too dear" indeed.

(He offers her a glass.)
Brandy?

SCENE 3

Sallie and Charlotte are in her nearly empty dressing room, packing traveling cases.

SALLIE. Well, that's the last of it.

CHARLOTTE. A whole life, packed into a few suitcases.

SALLIE. I've booked us tickets to the Channel port from Victoria Station.

CHARLOTTE. And then?

SALLIE. A ferry to another train, then Paris.

CHARLOTTE. Tomorrow?

SALLIE. Tonight.

CHARLOTTE. That's it then. So much for London.

SALLIE. I'll miss it too. Except the food. I'll be happy to never see another herring.

CHARLOTTE. You don't have to come, you know.

SALLIE. Don't be stupid. Of course I'm coming.

CHARLOTTE. I can't promise you work, Sallie.

SALLIE. We'll make work.

CHARLOTTE. I don't know how. I haven't done anything else since I was sixteen.

SALLIE. It's a new city. You'll act. I have an incredible idea for a production of Merchant. You've never played Shylock–

CHARLOTTE. I can't. You know I can't.

SALLIE. All right, you need a break. We'll take a break.

CHARLOTTE. Listen to me.

SALLIE. It will be like that time in New Orleans, remember? When we arrived in town and the theatre had closed? No one had thought to tell us.

CHARLOTTE. I wasn't a disgraced nobody in New Orleans.

SALLIE. We had so much fun with all that free time, just you and I. Until you met that red-haired governess, anyway. It's been an age since we had a vacation together.

CHARLOTTE. This isn't a vacation, it's exile.

SALLIE. We'll find our way.

CHARLOTTE. And what if we don't? You're used to me being rich and famous, not destitute and infamous.

SALLIE. So what?

CHARLOTTE. There's no reason for you to stay if there's no work. If there are no more plays, no more bookings, no more liaisons. If I'm no longer Charlotte Cushman. We have no more use for each other. You work for me. That's all.

SALLIE. *(exploding)* That's it! I'm sick of your shit!

CHARLOTTE. Excuse me!

SALLIE. You won't stop until you've pushed away every single person who loves you!

CHARLOTTE. Ugh, I'm so tired of talking about love.

SALLIE. I've kept your secrets! Polished your performances! Kept your name in the papers for the right reasons and out of them for the wrong ones! The least you can do is acknowledge what we mean to each other!

CHARLOTTE. And what is that?

SALLIE. *(furiously)* I'm your friend, you insufferable narcissist! Your dearest friend! And you're mine!

CHARLOTTE. Friendship has nothing to do with this. I'm finished.

SALLIE. You don't GET to give up! This is my life too! My vocation!

CHARLOTTE, What vocation? No one even knows who Sallie Mercer is! I've taken your ideas and claimed them as my own. Why wouldn't you rid yourself of such a parasite?

SALLIE. Because it's not about recognition for me, Charlotte! I don't need applause, or my name in print, or a parade like you do! I just want to do the plays!

CHARLOTTE. So do them.

SALLIE. If I could do this work without you, I would! I would have done it years ago!

(A moment as Charlotte takes this in, and Sallie realizes she's said it.)

I need the theatre. You've infected me with it, and now I can't live without it, and so I can't live without you. You don't get to throw away everything we've built– what I've built for you–because you feel ashamed. You owe me resilience.

CHARLOTTE. You believe I only think of myself. And sometimes you're right. Most of the time. But Sallie… Once the truth about me is revealed–I know what could happen to you.

SALLIE. Oh.

CHARLOTTE. Whatever becomes of me, if anyone suspects you of–anything–for being close to me–

SALLIE. I see.

CHARLOTTE. It will be that much worse for you. Unthinkably worse. I can survive my own humiliation, but not your–*(she can't say it.)* You must get far away from me.

SALLIE. I've always been in charge of my own destiny. When I entered your employ, when I learned who you are and who you love, when I made you realize that my vision would make you great–every step of the way, I've decided for myself what my life would look like. As much as any woman can. And I'm choosing to suffer your company, and to keep doing our work, no matter what.

CHARLOTTE. But at what risk?

SALLIE. I'm in, Charlotte. Sink or swim, we do it together. At least it won't be boring. Now, get it together. And don't try to make decisions for me again.

(A pause.)

CHARLOTTE. You know, no one else ever tells me what to do. They wouldn't dare.

SALLIE. No one else has to tolerate you day in and day out, either. We'll both cope. Whether we like it or not, we're all we've got now.

CHARLOTTE. Well…

SALLIE. Well what?

CHARLOTTE. You may need to get one more train ticket.

ELEANORA. *(fluttering into the room)* I got your note. But I haven't much time.

SALLIE. *(to Charlotte)* Really?

CHARLOTTE. I have needs.

SALLIE. Oh I know. The walls in New Orleans were thin and the ginger governess was loud. I'll…. check the flat one last time. (she nods to Eleanora) Miss.

ELEANORA. Oh hello!

CHARLOTTE. Sink or swim, Sallie.

SALLIE. *(as she leaves)* Keep paddling, Miss Cushman.

ELEANORA. Oh Charlotte, I've read the papers, it's all so horrible. The play–it's really canceled?

CHARLOTTE. I'm afraid so, pet.

ELEANORA, How dreadful! I was so looking forward to it.

CHARLOTTE. More than that–and the reason I asked you here–I'm leaving London. For good.

ELEANORA. Oh no! But why?

CHARLOTTE. It's what's best. These sorts of scandals–they're ruinous. And there are certain parties from whom I won't be safe until I'm in another country altogether.

ELEANORA. Poor you!

CHARLOTTE. Well, hopefully not so poor. How would you like to come with me? To Paris.

ELEANORA. Oh, Charlotte…

CHARLOTTE. You. Me. The Seine. What could be more romantic?

ELEANORA. I can't.

CHARLOTTE. Oh, I know it's sudden, but it will be an adventure!

ELEANORA. No, I mean I really can't. I'm engaged.

CHARLOTTE. Engaged!

ELEANORA. Yes.

CHARLOTTE. To be married?

ELEANORA. Yes!

CHARLOTTE. Since when? To whom?

ELEANORA. A very lovely gentleman, a Mister Hunt. He's asked me several times and I… well… my mother and I both thought it best that I accepted last night. After the chatter in the papers.

CHARLOTTE. I see.

ELEANORA. Mother was… concerned that we'd been spending rather too much time together. It didn't look right. Considering.

(Charlotte stares at her stonily.)

He's very nice.

CHARLOTTE. He's a he.

ELEANORA. Well… of course. What else do you expect? Ladies can't marry each other.

CHARLOTTE. You're lying to yourself. And to that 'very nice' gentleman.

ELEANORA. I most certainly am not! I am going to be a wife and a mother and a proper lady. And Albert–ah, Alfred?–Mister Hunt–will make a fine husband. You and I–we were just having a bit of fun.

CHARLOTTE. And now you're rushing into a sham engagement to distance yourself from a debauched pariah!

ELEANORA. You always use big words when you get cross.

CHARLOTTE. All of this happened because of you, you foolish little girl.

ELEANORA. Now you're just being mean.

CHARLOTTE. Where is your loyalty? Your constancy?

ELEANORA. You're behaving as if you didn't use me the entire time.

CHARLOTTE. Use you!

ELEANORA. Did you ever intend to bring me on as Juliet? Really?

(Charlotte is silent.)

Of course you didn't. And I never intended to throw my life away and leave polite society behind for a woman I barely know and who doesn't care for me a bit.

CHARLOTTE. You're abandoning me when I need you most.

ELEANORA. I never promised you anything. You're famous and I'm beautiful. We each got what we wanted, for a time. That's all.

CHARLOTTE. Well. Not so naive after all, pet.

(She smiles at her ruefully.)

You'll make a lovely bride.

ELEANORA. I know.

(She moves to leave, then stops.)

Oh. And I'm sorry about your sister. I guess she really is just as awful as you said.

CHARLOTTE. Susan? What about her?

ELEANORA. Oh dear. She didn't even tell you?

CHARLOTTE. What?

ELEANORA. Oh, this is awkward. Well. I heard from my cousin, who heard from her school friend, who heard from her brother who works at the Princess's Theatre–

CHARLOTTE. The Princess's!

ELEANORA. –that your sister has offered to collaborate with Edwin Forrest. She was spotted there today.

CHARLOTTE. With Forrest! She would never.

ELEANORA. I'm aware that you and Mister Forrest have less than cordial relations. But perhaps it's best for her. Women do well beside a strong man.

CHARLOTTE. I wouldn't know.

ELEANORA, No. I suppose you wouldn't.

(She kisses Charlotte on the cheek.)

Goodbye, Miss Cushman. Thank you for the acting lessons. I shall never forget them.

CHARLOTTE. Me neither.

(Eleanora smiles and exits.)

How could she? Treacherous, spineless, deceiving, faithless betrayer!

SALLIE. *(entering)* Mistress featherbrain won't be joining us?

CHARLOTTE. No! I mean, she won't. But that's not it. It's

worse!

SALLIE. I can't say I'm disappointed. She was dull as dirt.

CHARLOTTE. Aren't you listening? It's Susan!

SALLIE. What's Susan?

CHARLOTTE. She's… double-crossed me. Us. She's working with Forrest.

SALLIE. No! I don't believe it.

CHARLOTTE. Have you seen her today?

SALLIE. Not since early this morning.

CHARLOTTE. She's not at the flat?

SALLIE. No.

CHARLOTTE. Or in the dressing room.

SALLIE. No.

CHARLOTTE

I gave her every opportunity she ever had. If it wasn't for me, she'd still be working in our mother's boarding house, elbow deep in dirty dishwater! And the moment our circumstances reverse–! This, this is why I expect the worst from people, Sallie. They always deliver.

SALLIE. She didn't even say goodbye?

CHARLOTTE. Not a word.

SALLIE. Perhaps something has happened to her. She can't have really left.

CHARLOTTE. You're just angry that I'm right.

SALLIE. That's true. I do hate it when that happens.

SCENE 4

*Forrest and Susan are laughing, sipping brandy,
very cozy in his dressing room.*

FORREST.   …so there he was–genteel Macready–the picture of the effeminate aristocrat–

SUSAN. Mmm-hmm.

FORREST. –just the softest, weakest personation of a king you could imagine: *(lisping Britishly)* "for he that sheds his blood with me shall be my brother." As if such a feeble creature as he could lead a battle! I was ready to shout down my censure from the opera box–

SUSAN. Ooh, What did you say!

FORREST. I didn't have to. What do you think was hurled onto the stage from the opposite box?

SUSAN. I couldn't guess. Rotten fruit?

FORREST. A dead sheep! Right on the bastard! Baaaah!

SUSAN. Oh no!

FORREST. Oh yes! He never saw it coming. Nearly jumped out of his skin!

SUSAN. *(laughing)* I would have died!

FORREST. And when I went on as Henry the next weekend, the same audiences cheered me!

SUSAN. Rightly so.

FORREST. Here in London it's McCready, McCready, McCready. But New York sees right through him. That pretty poetry, the mincing about. They know that if Shakespeare were alive today, he would be an American!

SUSAN. At least at heart.

FORREST. Right you are.

(They toast.)

Now my dear, while I'm enjoying this stimulating conversation–

SUSAN. As am I.

FORREST. –shouldn't we discuss the matter at hand?

SUSAN. Which is?

FORREST. Mounting a new Romeo and Juliet. You and I.

SUSAN. Oh, but there's plenty of time for business. I'm just so enjoying getting to know you–

FORREST. Not the callow brute your sister made me out to be, eh?

SUSAN. Not a bit! And it's so nice to be in the company of a man, at long last.

FORREST. Poor thing. She's been keeping you locked away in her tower this whole time? A lovely young bit of raspberry like you?

SUSAN. Well, I was here to work…

FORREST. All that will change with me. You'll see. Meeting people– parties and dinners and dances–it's part of the work. She should have shown you all of it. But it's no surprise that she kept you from the other sex, given her… proclivities.

SUSAN. Enough about her.

FORREST. How the two of you are sisters I've no idea. You're such a sweet, delicate little thing–

SUSAN. Oh, stop…

FORREST. –and she, a galumphing ox! You really got the

lucky draw.

SUSAN. Well. I don't know.

FORREST. Lovely and modest. A winning combination in a woman.

(He refills both their glasses.)

Romeo and Juliet will be easy. Two attractive people, a cut-down script–

SUSAN. Cut down?

FORREST. Less Mercutio for one thing. Always a scene-stealer.

SUSAN. What else?

FORREST. Too much comedy in the beginning. Get rid of that. Focus on the lovers. And of course simplify Juliet.

SUSAN. Simplify her?

FORREST. She goes on and on with the damn nurse! So much talk, talk, talk. We only really need to hear her in her scenes with Romeo, and when it's time to die. It's been done that way, with actor's prompts, for a hundred years.

SUSAN. Fascinating!

FORREST. Audiences come for the big moments. The meat. They don't want to sit through the rest. You'll see.

SUSAN. It certainly does sound… simpler.

FORREST. It will be. A pretty creature like you, all you have to do is walk onstage and they'll love you. The fellows especially. And without the distraction of the other one, you'll be a star in your own right. The cream rises to the top, Miss Cushman.

SUSAN. *(flirtatiously)* Oh, is that how you've… risen?

FORREST. In a way.

SUSAN. Well, come on. I want to hear all about how the "first great American actor" got his start.

FORREST. Nitrous.

SUSAN. What?

FORREST. I was living in Philadelphia, working as a ship chandler–

SUSAN. How I love a gentleman who works with his hands!

FORREST. And I attended a scientific lecture, during which I volunteered to participate in an experiment on the effects of nitrous oxide–

SUSAN. You were–

FORREST. High as a kite. And in my addled state, a soliloquy came bursting forth–"Was ever woman in this humour woo'd? Was ever woman in this humour won? I'll have her, but I will not keep her long...."

SUSAN. Oh, is that–?

FORREST. Richard III. And another fellow attending the lecture–very well connected–was so impressed by my raw talent and animal magnetism, undeniable even under the influence of the gas, that he arranged an audition for me at Walnut Street.

SUSAN. And the rest is history.

FORREST. So it is.

(Clears his throat.)

Now, as for your own 'history'...

SUSAN. Hmm?

FORREST. Your little "incident".

SUSAN. Incident? *(realizing)* You mean Ned.

FORREST. Is there any way that you could send him home to your mother for a bit? Just to free you for more social engagements, perhaps discourage any more talk like that unfortunate piece in last week's paper?

SUSAN. You think I should send my son away?

FORREST. It would be wise. Just until you're married again.

Young unmarried actresses are always suspect, and with a child… it appears unseemly.

SUSAN. Perhaps you're right. Goodness knows being a mother is decidedly less glamorous than being an actress. If I leave both Charlotte and Ned behind, I can have a truly fresh start.

FORREST. Smart girl.

SUSAN. Honestly, I'm surprised you received me at all after that nasty article. It was so humiliating.

FORREST. Don't give it a second thought, Miss. I'm nothing if not understanding. And everyone deserves a second chance.

SUSAN. You really are kind. Charlotte was so wrong about you. She and I are like oil and water, always arguing, but you and I seem more… suited. As artistic partners.

FORREST. Does that surprise you?

SUSAN. Perhaps a bit. I wasn't sure we'd like each other.

FORREST. And now?

SUSAN. I'm quite certain that we do. Or, that I like you, at least. I feel I can truly be myself around you.

FORREST. You can.

SUSAN. And I can even… confide in you?

FORREST. I'm all ears, miss.

SUSAN. It's something of a relief. Charlotte being exposed. I had no idea about her assignations, her sickness–

FORREST. Poor thing, how could you? We all thought she was merely celibate. We couldn't have imagined… this.

SUSAN. No one ever spoke of me but in comparison to her, and always lacking. Pretty Susan, nice to look at, but 'without the spark of her sister's genius'. That was from my very first notice, for the Bride of Genoa. I never forgot that phrase. I was always to be only Charlotte Cushman's sister.

FORREST. But now?

SUSAN. She'll be gone, and people might see me for who I am without having someone to measure me against all the time. In a strange way I feel almost… grateful.

(She looks away.)

Am I a terrible person? For feeling such relief at my sister's misfortune?

FORREST. You dear girl. No, no, no. What you're feeling is perfectly natural. And your star will rise, and burn as brightly as hers ever did. Brighter.

SUSAN. But what if she doesn't leave? What if she tries to fight the rumors as libel, hold on to her place? I can't bear to go on being just the lesser Cushman.

FORREST. She can't. You won't!

SUSAN. *(holding back tears)* But how do you know?

FORREST. Because I have these.

(He retrieves Charlotte's letters from a hiding place.)

These letters will keep you safe, Susan. They prove that she's–what she is. And when I have them printed tonight, she'll be out of both our lives for good.

SUSAN. Oh, Mister Forrest!

FORREST. Edwin, please.

SUSAN. Are these real? Where did you get them?

FORREST. Never mind that. All that matters is that I have the means to give you everything you've ever wanted. Your own career. A place in the sun. Perhaps even a husband, if you'll have me.

SUSAN. Edwin!

FORREST. I may be forward. But I'm a man who knows his own desires. And how can you blame me, Susan. You're so beautiful, and the two of us so alike…

SUSAN. But–aren't you married?

FORREST. That wilting English Rose? She's been having assignations of her own. Making a fool of me with some limey actor.

SUSAN. Poor man! I'm so sorry.

FORREST. Don't be. I'd rather an American Beauty. I'm filing for divorce as soon as I return to Philadelphia, and then we'll be wed.

SUSAN. This is all happening so fast!

FORREST. Don't you see? We're so much the same. Both mistreated in our first marriages. Both encumbered by your disgraceful sister. Both destined for greatness. We're meant to be together.

SUSAN. *(swooning, she collapses into his arms)* Oh! I'm so sorry! I get so overwhelmed!

FORREST. *(producing smelling salts, stroking her hair)* There there. You dear thing. I don't mean to rush you. I can be patient. But I want you to know how it feels to be taken care of by a real man.

SUSAN. That's all I've ever wanted.

FORREST. Let's get these letters to the printers, and we'll celebrate your freedom. Your fresh start.

SUSAN. You would do that for me?

FORREST. All that and more.

   (They kiss.)

SCENE 5

Sallie is sweeping the bare stage. Charlotte sits on a crate.

SALLIE. Just a few hours until the train.

(Charlotte doesn't speak.)

We have to return the keys to Mister Webster, but I haven't seen him since last night. Have you?

(No answer.)

Well, we can always leave them in the dressing room. Do you have a book for the ride? I was thinking of rereading Candide. Just to get in a French frame of mind.

(Still no answer.)

She may still come back, Miss. There's time.

CHARLOTTE. You know, when I first became an actress, she came to see me, in Albany. That was my first Romeo. I was… nineteen? God, was I ever so young? And John Nickinson–remember him?

SALLIE. The Canadian? He named his daughter after you.

CHARLOTTE. He was my Friar Lawrence. Manager at the time. He led me onstage at the end of the first performance and he placed a wreath of flowers on my head. Like he was crowning me as an heir to the American stage. And Susan was there, in the front row, gazing up at me with such admiration–this thirteen year old girl who had never understood me–and I thought… this is how it feels to be seen. This is how I will be happy.

(A pause.)

All gone now. The stage, the poetry, the sense of purpose. My laurel crown ripped away and set ablaze by Edwin fucking Forrest. And my sister by his side, warming her hands at the fire.

SALLIE. Yes, it's all very tragic and terribly unfair and you're the most ill-treated woman who's ever lived.

CHARLOTTE. Don't mock me.

SALLIE. You can mope forever or you can move forward. And in this case, forward is a train to Paris, leaving in two hours from Victoria's Station. And I promise you, I will not listen to you monologize for the entire ride.

CHARLOTTE. You prefer Voltaire to your 'dearest friend'?

SALLIE. No contest.

CHARLOTTE. Fair enough.

(They hear a moan from the vom, or a trap – somewhere onstage but unseen)

SALLIE. What was that?

WEBSTER. *(moaning louder)* Ohhhhhh…. Who's there?

CHARLOTTE. Mister Webster?

SALLIE. Are you all right?

(Together they help him unsteadily to his feet.)

WEBSTER. If I never see another drop of gin, it will be too soon.

SALLIE. Here, up you go…

CHARLOTTE. He's practically pickled.

WEBSTER. Occupational hazard of the manager's job. Did I…. say anything last night? I tend to get a touch… too direct. When I've had some drink.

(Charlotte and Sallie look at each other.)

SALLIE. Not a thing, Mister Webster.

CHARLOTTE. You remained the perfect gentleman.

WEBSTER. Well, that's a relief. I'd hate to think that I compounded the indignity of your ordeal.

(He pats his pockets.)

I feel as if I've forgotten something.

SALLIE. Here are the keys to the theatre, sir.

WEBSTER. Oh, no, not that…

CHARLOTTE. And the flat.

WEBSTER. There was something else.

(He rolls unsteadily, hiccups and swallows, looking sick.)

Please excuse me, ladies. I must… I'll be back.

(He lurches off.)

SALLIE. If he doesn't make it, you're cleaning up after him.

CHARLOTTE. If that's what twenty more years in the theatre does to you, perhaps I'm getting off easy.

(They laugh.)

We were supposed to have a packed house here in just a few hours. Now look at it. Is there anything sadder than an empty theatre?

MATILDA. *(appearing at the back of the house)* Only me. Terribly sad, humbled, and filled with regret.

SALLIE. *(To Charlotte)* Miss?

CHARLOTTE. Give us the room, please, Sallie.

SALLIE. Yes, Miss Cushman. I'll be close by. If anyone needs me.

(Sallie glares at Matilda as she exits. A silence.)

CHARLOTTE. Quite the article you wrote.

MATILDA. It was horrible, what I did. Unforgivable.

CHARLOTTE. Yes.

MATILDA. But it was also horrible what YOU did! I was hurt. Jealous. Wretched!

CHARLOTTE. If you think that my–dalliance, or whatever you want to call it, is somehow equal to the wreckage that you've caused–

MATILDA. I'm trying to apologize. I'm sorry. I'm SORRY! I was a vengeful, short-sighted fool.

CHARLOTTE. It doesn't matter now.

MATILDA. But of course it matters! I love you!

CHARLOTTE. I'm leaving London for good, because I've been exposed. Exposed by your hit piece!

MATILDA. I… wrote a retraction. In hopes that it might help. Dismissed it all as evening wheezes from an envious rival. But…

CHARLOTTE. But what?

MATILDA. Edwin Forrest still has the letters. Our letters.

CHARLOTTE. Ah.

MATILDA. And he's printing them tonight.

CHARLOTTE. The final nail in my coffin.

MATILDA. Oh, Charlotte, I tried to get them back! I really did! But I couldn't and now it's all ruined.

CHARLOTTE. You know, Max… I think I really did love you. I do. But you could never have loved me.

MATILDA. What do you mean? Of course I love you!

CHARLOTTE. I don't think that I let you. And that's my fault.

MATILDA. No. Let me come with you. Wherever you're going. We can make a new life, together.

CHARLOTTE. Matilda...

MATILDA. Look at me. I'm on my knees. Begging for your forgiveness. Please.

CHARLOTTE. You can't trust me, and I can't trust you.

What's left to salvage? What are you even fighting for? *(Sallie and Webster enter. Webster sees the two and flushes, turning around and clearing his throat. The two women leap to their feet.)*

SALLIE. Sorry to interrupt, but I think this might be important.

CHARLOTTE. What?

WEBSTER. This.

(He produces a bouquet.)

Early this morning, I awoke, briefly to, ah, settle my stomach. I ran into your sister–

CHARLOTTE. And? What did the petticoat Judas have to say?

WEBSTER. I was in quite a rush, to, you know… so she just gave me this and insisted that I get it to you the moment I saw you. But in my state, I'm afraid I left it in the water closet.

(He gives it to her.)

So sorry, Miss.

MATILDA. Flowers? From Susan? Strange.

SALLIE. Not if you look closely.

(Charlotte understands.)

CHARLOTTE. There's…. Fennel.

SALLIE. For flattery.

MATILDA. Snapdragon for… deception?

SALLIE. Yes. And violets.

CHARLOTTE. For loyalty. Devotion.

SALLIE. Now do you see?

WEBSTER. See what?

CHARLOTTE. She didn't leave me. Whatever she's doing with Forrest–

SALLIE. –is a trick. A ruse to get close to him.

MATILDA. But what's this last one?

CHARLOTTE. It's… a black-eyed Susan.

WEBSTER. And what does that mean?

SUSAN. *(appearing with the letters in hand)* Justice.

CHARLOTTE. Suzy!

(Charlotte moves to embrace Susan, who cooly rebuffs her, holding out the letters.)

SUSAN. I believe these are yours?

CHARLOTTE. Susan, I'm so–

MATILDA. But how did you do it? How did you get the letters?

SUSAN. It turns out that both Cushmans are rather convincing actresses. And I do have a bit of practice at showing men what they want to see.

SALLIE. You didn't…

SUSAN. No! No. I just let him think that we might, and then I hit him over the head with a vase on his dressing table. Solid thing.

WEBSTER. Well. I am sorry. For misplacing Miss Cushman's gift, and for… *(he clears his throat)* I'm wondering if–perhaps we might–

SALLIE. Do you think it might be worth re-erecting the set, Mister Webster?

WEBSTER. I do, quite. I suspect that Miss Hays' retraction might have done the trick. And Miss Cushman's audience may be less fickle than I'd feared.

CHARLOTTE. But what if they don't come?

SALLIE. And what if they do?

MATILDA. It's worth a go, at least!

WEBSTER. Faith, Miss Cushman! We must have faith to survive this mad business. Miss Mercer–unpack the costumes! I'll gather some stagehands to get the set back up. We only have an hour or so.

(He points to Matilda.)

You–can you use a hammer?

MATILDA. I, uh–

(She looks at Charlotte.)

I can do whatever you need. For as long as you want me to. I am but a penitent.

WEBSTER. Erm, well, that won't be necessary, Miss. Perhaps just some light carpentry. This way.

MATILDA. Charlotte?

CHARLOTTE. On your way, Miss Hays.

(They leave.)

Susan. I–

SUSAN. You don't have to say it.

CHARLOTTE. You saved me. You did. The debt I owe you–

SUSAN. Come on, we shouldn't leave all this to Mr. Webster and Miss Mercer, don't you think?

(They begin to rebuild the set—lifting flats, hanging drapes, moving chairs, the world of Romeo & Juliet slowly reappearing. Something is being repaired.)

CHARLOTTE. About... what I said.

SUSAN. Don't. Please.

(She struggles with a flat or drape.)

Oof, this is heavy.

CHARLOTTE. Let me.

(She helps her.)

I didn't mean it. When I said that you–

SUSAN. You know, all my life I just wanted you to like me. And all my life I've known that you didn't.

CHARLOTTE. Susan–

SUSAN. Let me finish. I remember you watching me play with my dolls, looking at me with your eyebrows knit together. And you said–

CHARLOTTE. *(remembering)* "It must be terribly boring to be a girl."

SUSAN. As if you were a different species!

CHARLOTTE. Aren't I?

SUSAN. And then, later... you smashed them! All my dolls! That's how stupid you found the whole enterprise. And me.

CHARLOTTE. That's not the reason!

SUSAN. It's all right, Charlotte.

CHARLOTTE. It's not! I wasn't judging you, or the dolls. I was just trying to understand! You. Girls. I... smashed the doll's heads open so I could see what they were thinking.

(A pause–and they collapse into laughter. A release. A thaw.)

SUSAN, *(recovering)* Better their heads than mine, I guess!

CHARLOTTE. God, I still don't get it! Womanhood's never fit me. It's like a pair of shoes that's a size too small.

SUSAN. Fancy shoes always do hurt a bit.

CHARLOTTE. And it fits you so well, Susan. Like it was made for you. It was easier to act like you were shallow than admit how jealous I was.

SUSAN. You! Jealous of me!

CHARLOTTE. I'm not a good woman. Playing opera and Shakespeare's as natural as breathing compared to the role of the docile young lady.

SUSAN. And when you play the breeches parts–

CHARLOTTE. It's easier still. Because as Romeo, I can be something I never can in life.

SUSAN. A man?

CHARLOTTE. Something closer to myself. The stage–it's

the only place where people actually like… what I am.

SUSAN. You're an idiot.

CHARLOTTE. Excuse me?

SUSAN. After all this, you still think that hiding in life and being who you really are on stage makes sense?

CHARLOTTE. To be fair, you just went to extraordinary lengths to help me keep that part of myself in the shadows.

SUSAN. Light, shadow, onstage or off, breeches or skirts– it's all you, Charlotte. And it's all wonderful. My wonderful big sister.

(Charlotte, for once, is speechless.)

And for what it's worth, I don't care a bit that you love ladies. God knows loving men hasn't worked out spectacularly for me. Did you love Miss Hays? Matilda?

CHARLOTTE. Not wisely or well.

SUSAN. But why in the world would she publish this horrid gossip?

CHARLOTTE, "Charlotte Cushman's Unnatural Loves"?

SUSAN. If she's your… paramour?

CHARLOTTE. Because, as I said… I'm not a good woman.

(She sighs.)

I deserved her scorn. But she's hurt me beyond forgiveness.

SUSAN. Surely you can find some way to reconcile. She seems contrite. Why not call it even?

CHARLOTTE. Matilda and I have spent years getting even with one another. But this was a step too far. Retraction or not, handing over our letters gave Forrest ammunition in ink.

SUSAN. He's vile. Pretending to find him charming was the best acting I've ever done in my life.

CHARLOTTE. Thank god it was just a one-night engagement.

SUSAN. I still don't understand why he hates you so much.

CHARLOTTE. Because I look better in pants.

(As they laugh, a loud bang as Forrest, his head wrapped in bandages, barges in the door)

FORREST. Where are they?!

CHARLOTTE. Oh, right on cue, Mister Forrest!

SUSAN. Here we are! Perhaps your vision is still a bit blurred? How's your head?

FORREST. Cushman! Foul she-devil!

CHARLOTTE & SUSAN. Which one?

FORREST. BOTH of you! Two peas in a pod, aren't you? The unnatural shrew and the duplicitous strumpet!

CHARLOTTE. Ooh, perhaps that should go on our next handbill?

SUSAN. It does have a nice ring to it.

FORREST. The English are too stupid to see your foulness or my greatness. This city doesn't deserve me. Good riddance! You can have it!

CHARLOTTE. Aw, closing Othello so soon?

FORREST. I'll reopen in Philadelphia, or New York! Where they have taste, and know a star when they see him! And I'll happily never lay eyes on you miserable hags again.

SUSAN. It's probably for the best. We're simply too alike to work together.

FORREST. You! You're even worse than her. And don't flatter yourself–I never wanted you to begin with. I'd never have lowered myself to wed a divorcee-slut with a bastard child!

(Charlotte slaps him, hard. He reels. Impulsively, he grabs a prop sword lying on the stage.)

That's it! You think yourself a man, Cushman? Then let's settle this as men. Turn and draw, you cunt!

CHARLOTTE. Villain. You know not what you do. Susan, my sword.

SUSAN. Charlotte, don't!

CHARLOTTE. He's impugned your honor for the last time. I'll shut that venom-spewing mouth for good.

(She raises her sword.)

Have at thee, coward!

(They fight.)

FORREST. I'll kill you if you don't yield.

CHARLOTTE. The swords are foils, Forrest.

FORREST. No matter. I've practiced strangling a woman to death every night.

CHARLOTTE. And I've practiced stabbing swaggering men.

(Fighting continues. Webster enters)

WEBSTER. We'll need another pair of hands to re-hang the–

(He sees them.)

I'll… I'll come back.

(He scurries off.)

CHARLOTTE. You know, Edwin, given the way you wield a sword, you might rather try your hand at women's parts.

FORREST. I'll have your parts hacked off.

CHARLOTTE. Not fighting like that, you won't.

FORREST. Usurper! Look upon thy death.

CHARLOTTE. *(to Susan)* You know what they say: he that dies pays all debts.

SUSAN. Stop this! Enough!

FORREST. Surrender, Cushman! Or taste my blade!

CHARLOTTE. No metal can bear half the keenness of thy sharp envy.

FORREST. I detest you.

CHARLOTTE. And I pity you.

FORREST. RAAAAHHHH!

(He charges her, and she finally disarms him, her foot on his chest and her sword at his throat.)

They'll all forget you! Once they know who you really are, once they truly understand the depths of your depravity, they'll erase you forever, and only I'll be left!

CHARLOTTE. I'd rather be truly great for a moment than remembered forever as a mediocrity.

FORREST. God damn you! And god damn your whore sister!

CHARLOTTE. I warned you what would happen if you dared insult my sister again. Didn't you decode my message?

SUSAN. Men are so slow to understand these things. And so easily manipulated.

(Webster, Matilda, and Sallie rush in.)

MATILDA. There's a line around the block full of patrons chanting your names, demanding to see Romeo and Juliet!

CHARLOTTE. Can it be?

WEBSTER. It's true! They're banging down the doors for the Cushman sisters!

SUSAN. We've saved!

SALLIE. I told you so!

(She looks down at Forrest, still on the floor.)

Oh, hello Mister Forrest!

MATILDA. Nice to see you again. Shall we continue our conversation about the dominant sex?

CHARLOTTE. Oh, I may have a few notions to contribute!

SUSAN. Me too.

FORREST. A curse on your production! I'll be revenged on all of you! The English! Actresses! Women! The whole pack of you!

(He limps out.)

CHARLOTTE. I've wanted to do that for a long time.

SUSAN. It was glorious. And it certainly expunged a good portion of your debt.

CHARLOTTE. Thank God.

(She collapses.)

Tybalt's going to have it easy tonight.

WEBSTER. Ready yourselves, ladies. We don't have long. *(He scurries off.)*

MATILDA. Charlotte, I–

SALLIE. Come, Miss Hays. Let's give the Cushmans some time to prepare.

MATILDA. Yes. Of course. I'll be watching from the front row.

CHARLOTTE. *(warily)* All right.

(They leave.)

SUSAN. Honestly, this debt business is silly. You've got to stop thinking in terms of who owes whom, who's done more kindness and who's done more harm. Don't do it to me, and–perhaps–not to Miss Hays?

CHARLOTTE. You've become very bossy.

SUSAN. Just feeling confident in my area of expertise.

CHARLOTTE. Love?

SUSAN. It doesn't involve ledgers or debts. Mine doesn't. For you.

My bounty is as boundless as the sea, Charlotte.

(A pause, then Charlotte responds:)

CHARLOTTE. My love as deep.

SUSAN. The more I give to you, the more I have…

CHARLOTTE. For both are infinite.

> *(A beat; they look at each other. Ritualistically, they put on their costumes, helping each other with buttons and laces. They circle each other, touching palms.)*

Applause.

EPILOGUE

SALLIE. A kind of peace this opening awaked;
    As one, the sisters star rose ever higher
    And 'tween the two, where once a chasm gaped
    A bridge of love stands, forged in hardship's fire.
    We'll tomorrow get the rave reviews in
    For Charlotte's Romeo and her sister Sus–
CHARLOTTE. Sallie! Hurry up the epilogue, will you?
SALLIE. Don't rush me.
SUSAN. And that rhyme is terrible.
SALLIE. I'm almost done, I said!
    (aside) And Sallie's fate? I'll dwell in hist'ry not;
    For even as the future rushes hence,
    Extraordinary women are forgot.
    Adieu.

END OF PLAY

NOTES

(Use this space to make notes for your production)

NOTES

(Use this space to make notes for your production)

GATHER BY THE GHOST LIGHT is a storytelling podcast in radio theater format. Think of the Ghost Light as your campfire. Gather around and listen to stories from a variety of genres. Playwright Jonathan Cook and Devon McSherry are the hosts of the series and most of the stories you hear were originally written as stage plays and they now have been adapted to audio plays with professional voice actors and immersive sound effects. The audio dramas produced on this podcast give these talented playwrights an even wider audience for their stories. We welcome you to join us on this journey as we extend the voices of playwrights around the world!

Available wherever you get your podcasts!

For more information, please visit:

www.gatherbytheghostlight.com

Gather by the Ghost Light annual anthologies of audio plays produced on the podcast are all available through Ghost Light Publications!

Find more plays at

www.ghostlightpubs.com

9 781964 045146